infinite ending:

ten stories

Infinite Ending: Ten Stories

Published by Kykeon Media

Published December 2014

ISBN: 978-0-9834599-9-6

infinite ending:

ten stories

by Frank Marcopolos

Preface

"Write a story a month," Larah said. We were brunching on a picnic table outside Wheatsville, on South Lamar.

My mouth full of a Coolhaus Double Chocolate Chip Cookie + Dirty Mint Chip Ice Cream sandwich, I said, "Hmmm?"

"One story a month, January through October," Larah said. "Then publish it by December."

"You don't know how hard that would be," I said, swallowing. "Besides, there's football to watch, and beer to drink, and parties and shows and stuff. This is Austin! No one's gonna sit there and write a story a month while living in Austin."

"Oh," she said. "I thought you were a writer."

And so the gauntlet was thrown.

This 10-story collection of postmodern literary fiction is the result of that challenge, for better or worse. A story a month, all of them having been excruciatingly scrutinized by the infamous Austin Writing Workshop, and so...y'know. There's that. Deadlines do seem to work miracles for productivity, but they do not guarantee quality—only you can decide on that. So, I hope you enjoy reading them as much as I have enjoyed writing them.

I do realize that it can seem pretentious for an author to thank people, in a way, but I also have a feeling mixed in with that realization which seems to indicate that documented gratitude is in order here. I know that this book would not have been possible without the current and past members of the Austin Writing Workshop (at different times entitled the Real Writers Workshop and the Waterloo Writers Workshop): Jim S., Cory B., Michael W., Meghan W., Samira N., Theresa W., Kirsten D., Phillip D., Kara M., and everyone else who has been a workshop participant over the years. These members' critiques contributed significantly to these ten stories, and for that I will be eternally grateful.

It's also pretentious, I'm aware, for me to have included with the ten fictional pieces two essays about the literary genre of postmodernism. Nevertheless, they're here, and they are quite easily avoided if the pretentious factor is just too high for your liking. In my defense, the reason I have included them is to be helpful to those who may not be as knowledgeable about the topic as are others, and I do this despite the acknowledged risk of being thought ridiculously pretentious. So goes the world in which we live.

Others who must be thanked for their contribution to my life in general include the following: Bill Hicks, J.D. Salinger, Richard Ford, Marshall Mathers, Robert Bly, Paul Dobransky, David Simon, Raymond Carver, and Matt Nix.

For Bill Hicks and New Kids on the Block,forever playing from their—and in our—hearts.

Table of Contents

1.
Tock

The meat-packing district is trendy now. It didn't used to be. It used to be full of fat Italian guys smoking stubby cigarettes inside the cabs of loud, exhaust-belching, graffiti-stained trucks delivering meat. Now, every night of the week, networking parties rage inside spaces formerly used for the production of meat products. Socialites like Allie are often found, as she was now, standing with a crystal flute full of pink champagne in her dainty hand, greeting trust-funded hipsters before they enter the by-invite-only hot spot. The fat Italians are not invited. They're all in Hunts Point now, anyway—or, that's how it seems. The sad reality is that Then and Now, Here and There, it's all a hazy, white-noise blur.

Allie (by birth: "Aywalasha Rai") stood like the proper, finishing-school girl she was—obelisk-straight, her hair like black silk flowing over her dome-slope shoulders. Reconning the scene, Allie's perfect posture reminded me of 7th Street, that row of nearly identical Indian restaurants, where we tried to get Allie to give up the goods on three major players in a global money-laundering operation. She was standing that way all through the interrogation, never wavering under the pressure. We failed to get the information we needed out of her, but that doesn't mean I can't be nostalgic about it all. "What *drives* you, Peter?" Allie had whispered to me over tandoori chicken before the interrogation, in the kind of romantic, airy voice that can make even the rumbling New York City delivery trucks sound like Aeolian harps. Her perfect posture wind-swept into her sweet voice in my ear. That's one of those tricks of the mind that can seem cruel or kind, depending.

I looked at my watch. Twenty-one hundred hours. Almost time to go. The watch itself used to be quite handsome, years ago—a watch any man would be proud to wear in a Congressional hearing or out in the real world. Now, though, it's got little nicks everywhere, scratches on the black-metal band, tiny bits of grime along the rim of the face. Sure, it's distortion-free crystal with all kinds of high-tech features, but it still bears the wounds of time and high-risk ops. What happens when you successfully complete your training, well, one of the things anyway, is that they give you a thousand-dollar keepsake. This one was all shiny and awe-inspiring and manly back then. Now, it's all beat up and dirty. A rotting shame, really.

Allie, by contrast, wore a perfect, round, pink locket with a sterling silver edge on a chain around her neck. The locket, I knew, contained a creased, black-and-white photograph of her mother, who had complemented her daughter's elite education in New Delhi with comprehensive lessons about every faith on Earth, teaching the child early on about the true power of beliefs. "What," Allie had asked me over Shiraz and red velvet cupcakes, "or *who* has made you believe in these ideas? Freedom. Traitor. Justice. What are these things, really?"

I laughed when she said that that night. What else could I do, really? It was an uncomfortable laughter, but I cleverly covered its tracks by sipping some zesty wine. I smiled and held my brow in a sophisticated pose, joked about her "rhetorical games." But it stuck with me. It stuck with me. No matter how much I knew about emotional manipulation, sometimes simple truth broke through the defenses of my training, regardless.

Outside the meat-packing district warehouse-turned-rave, Allie's silky red dress rippled in the breeze, and I knew it was the same dress she wore to a gala at the Princess Hotel in Acapulco, a Beaujolais in her henna-adorned hand, her hair fixed into a braided ponytail. She knew it was the kind of dress that, on *her* body, manipulated men's minds in ways she could use. Even a trained operator has a hard time shaking primitive instincts. "Live in the eternal now, beyond all perceived dimensions and limitations," she had said over cocktails at the breezy hotel bar.

That was her response, her *answer*. I had asked her how I could possibly live in a time-relative world where everything was all jumbled together in four non-linear dimensions. I had made a joke about never being late for a meeting, and then that's what she said. Like I've been trying to explain, the lady is *trouble*.

At the time, though, I didn't realize just how much trouble she was. I thought she was just another rich girl, playing the traditional game of dialectical finance—funding the arts and other worthy causes on one hand, and shady, often violent, organizations on the other. But Allie was no ordinary target. Allie always had objectives all her own, and sometimes I thought I could see just a glimpse of the rot beneath the glittery surface.

I took her advice to heart, tried to live in the eternal now, as best as I could understand the concept. The real trouble came when my deep cover was blown after I confused all the god-damned dates and all the god-damned people and places. The alleged *facts*. I got mixed up about what had happened and when, what had happened to *me*. The big boys don't need operators who can't keep their stories straight, especially under their relatively mild interrogation techniques. I'm lucky to be alive, I guess. That's what they told me, anyway, before they kicked me out the frosted-glass door, burned.

Something in Allie's dark, dazzling eyes told me she knew I was here, not only back in New York, but right behind this wall, watching her. I got the feeling that, worse than not caring, she *enjoyed* it. She knew, somehow, that she had emerged victorious.

As I stood there, with hot dog wrappers and shredded coffee cups swirling near my feet, the smell of something unknowable but funky in the air, I thought that maybe it was all just another illusion, another crimson-tinted minefield mind fuck. Allie, I mean, and all of my time with her. My belly murmured, the bell for another dumpster dive. But before I could stop spying Allie, my Allie, my mind played one last trick on me. Sounding far away and echoic, it asked: Is love real?

2.

Conversing

For my son, Ocean.

A few months into 2012, I drove for two straight days, pretty much, down from Brooklyn to Austin, Texas. The indie A & R scene had dried up for me in New York, so I needed a new start. Austin, with its live music and South by Southwest and Keeping Itself Weird, seemed as good a place as any for a revival.

Katie Alpert was an actress who had been to L.A. three times, only to be forced back to Texas after each trip because she couldn't "catch her big break." Plus, she got homesick. Out in L.A., she told me, men she dated gave her things like emerald-and-diamond necklaces, completely paid-off Benzes, and marriage proposals. But she could never find a man (or woman) to offer her acting gigs, and so she made her way back to Austin and decided to start her own fitness-video company on the Internet.

One Saturday, thirty minutes late, Katie pulled her gleaming, red Mercedes SUV into a spot directly across from my second-floor apartment on South Lamar. I watched her from my balcony: she stepped out of the car while talking on her sleek pink cell phone, sunlight beaming off her large black sunglasses. Her white racerback tank's straps narrowed over her shoulders, which revealed stark-white tan lines on inflamed-pink skin. A dime-sized hole on left side of the bottom of the shirt revealed more of her sunburned skin.

When I got downstairs, Katie was leaning into the tailgate of the SUV, fiddling around with some things in the back of the car. I noticed that she had a small, faint, brown stain on the left side of the seat of her golden shorts. It was more faded on the outside of the stain than on the inside.

"Nice day, huh?" I said. A glint of sunshine reflected off Katie's wig clip on the back of her head. Most of the time you couldn't see the clip through her realistic, thick, cocoa-brown strands, but for some reason it was sticking out among the strands of faux hair, which ran down to the middle of her neck.

"Blue skies," she said, slamming the gate shut. "Hard to film, better for hiking."

I smiled at the film-industry reference. The way she said it, with a pleasant, high-pitched voice, made me glad to be with her, happy she had chosen to be with me. It reminded me of the feeling I got when we met at Star Bar on Sixth while watching a Cowboys playoff game. She was an animated fan, full of cheerleader vitality. At one point, she smiled at me while I was talking to someone else. I noticed it out of the corner of my eye, and I felt like there was a spark there. After a while, I gathered up enough liquid courage to talk to her. Katie liked the fact that I was in the music business. She seemed a little too into it, though, as if she thought I could help her get some acting roles or make lucrative contacts, which I couldn't. It troubled me some. But at the time I thought we'd work it out later, when we knew each other better.

Getting into the car now, I noticed the extent of the mess in back—a smattering of clothes, duffel bags, blankets, wood planks, and other things. "Your car kinda reminds me of hauling band gear to gigs in Alphabet City," I said. It was a line I used all the time, almost automatically. It usually got back questions about what being on the road with bands was like, whether there really are groupies, and other similar questions about the sex, drugs, and rock 'n' roll lifestyle.

"Yeah," Katie said. "It's usually better. I'm just going through some stuff at my house right now. Hey, you gotta sort things out, right? Know what I'm talking about?"

"Right," I said, despite not having any idea what she was talking about. "Like, what kinda stuff are you going through at your house?"

"Oh," she said. "Don't worry. Nothing big, no big deal."

"Sounds good," I said. I had an instinct to ask more questions, but I suppressed it. Whatever she had going on at her house, I decided, was her business. I should keep my nosiness out of it.

"Are you gonna wear that...is it a *trilby?*...the whole time?" Katie said, starting the vehicle. Her voice was clipped, terse, almost childish, but as if she had chosen to make it sound that way. "Not to be, like, one of those people. But that hat, it's not really, like, a hiking hat or whatever."

I felt a flash-pang of insecurity in my gut. I took the hat off and ran my fingers through my thinning, middle-aged hair. "Yeah," I said. "I just kinda grabbed it without thinking too much. I guess you're right. It's not exactly appropriate."

"You can toss it in back if you want," she said, seeing me holding the hat awkwardly.

"Toss it in back?" I said. After a momentary hesitation, I tossed it in back among the other debris.

She smiled, and I got the feeling she felt as though she had won something. "Do you know anywhere we could grab a breakfast taco?" Katie said. "I need to eat. I haven't had breakfast yet."

"Sure," I said. "Yeah. Ummm, we can hit up Torchy's right here on Lamar. Or a little more up the road there's a food truck place that's pretty good."

"Cool, let's go food truck," she said. I looked over, and I thought I noticed that Katie had faintly dark circles under her eyes, as if she hadn't slept much. It was hard to tell because of her sunglasses, but I was pretty sure.

We headed out of the apartment complex in hungry silence. I looked around the front of the vehicle. Bits of papers, CDs, combs, make-up cases, lipstick tubes, dust, Tic-Tac boxes, eyeglass cases, sunglasses, perfume bottles, dog-eared novels, and other items were scattered about. I picked up an overloaded slim CD case from the debris around my feet. There were five CDs in the case, albums by Isaac Shepherd, Def Leppard, Frank Sinatra, John Coltrane, and D12. "Music?" I said, trying to keep all the CDs in the case.

"Oh, look! We're here," Katie said. "Telepathy Tacos. We know what you want before you do. How quaint." She turned off Lamar and onto a dirt and gravel parking area adjacent to a T-Mobile store.

We got out of the car and walked up to the ordering window. "What can I get for y'all," said the guy in the truck.

Katie said, "Umm. Do y'all use raw-milk cheese?"

"No, just the regular," said the guy in the truck.

Katie said, "Okayyy, what about your eggs? Are they free-range organic? I don't like those cooped-up chicken eggs."

"Yes," the guy said, looking exasperated. "Sure."

"Okay, and your bacon? Is that organic also?" Katie said. "Nitrites'll kill you!"

"Yes, ma'am," said the guy in the truck "They come from organic piggies."

"Okay, I'll umm, lessee. I'll just have the southwest taco, but with none of that horrible cheese, please. Oh, and a small coffee with three sugars and a little cream, as well," Katie said. "But, really, y'all should really consider changing your menu to have the raw. I mean, it's 2012, not 1847."

"Yes, ma'am," the guy in the truck said, looking relieved that her order was complete.

Considering the look on the vendor's face, I ordered a pre-made and cellophane-wrapped brownie.

While Katie took a phone call, I wandered around toward the back of the food truck. The door was half-open. Admittedly, I could have seen it wrong, but it seemed like the guy who took our orders was picking his nose and mixing it in Katie's food.

When we got back into the car, Katie said, "I think I might have to file a health complaint against that food truck."

I said, "Um, you might not wanna eat that, actually."

"Why not?" she said, unwrapping the taco. "I'm starving."

"Well, I'm not sure," I said. "But..."

She chomped into the taco lustily.

I said, "I think that guy might have put some, uh, special sauce in your food."

Chewing she said, "Ah, no way, dude. You probably saw God knows what. Do y'all eat breakfast tacos in New York?"

"It's not a big thing, no," I said. "Bagels and lox are more of a New York thing, actually. Maybe a donut from a street cart."

"I remember this one time when I was out in Hollywood, we were having breakfast, my girlfriends and me, and these guys that we knew came over and joined us. Except there's this one guy and he's new to us. Never seen him before, right? And so anyway, he's sitting next to me, and we get to talking and I tell him that at one point I was living in Vegas. And *he* says—are you ready for this?"

"Yeah, sure."

"He says, he goes, 'Were you a stripper?' Just like that, right out in front of everybody like that. Just like that. Can you believe that shit? Isn't that unbelievable?"

"Uhhhh."

"And I never forgave that guy. Tim was his name. I always called him Dim Tim after that. He's still friends with all my girlfriends, but I don't *ever* talk to him. And I *never* will, either."

"Never?"

"Never."

"Did he ever apologize to you? This Dim Tim guy?"

"Oh yeah, sure," she said. "About a million times."

"He did?"

"Yeah."

"And you still won't forgive him?" I said.

"Never," she said. "I don't think it's right to embarrass me in front of everyone like that. That guy doesn't deserve grace."

Seeing how strong her feelings were about it, I decided not to argue the point. I said, over-enthusiastically, "I think you're right to do that. He has no right. No right!"

"Damn skippy!"

I said, "So, I guess I shouldn't make any stripper jokes around you, then?"

She smiled. "Prolly a good idea, yeah."

"I'll go toss these in the trash," I said about the breakfast garbage.

"You could just toss it in back, but whatever," she said.

I laughed, but she was serious. I froze for a second. Then I tossed it in back.

When we got to the parking lot for the hiking trail, Katie lowered the tailgate of the car to change into her sneakers. Her cell's ring tone, the '80s hit song "8675-309," went off. Her phone, I now noticed, had faded edges and small chips in the pink paint. She looked at it, smiled at me, and took the call. She walked away, talking into the cell.

I sat on the tailgate for about fifteen minutes as Katie wandered out of earshot, barefoot. I looked inside the car at the debris she had back there. Naked Barbie dolls missing limbs, a pair of six-inch Lucite heels, a one-eyed teddy bear with cigarette burns on it, and a small doll house with no doors caught my eye. "Quite the collection of totems," I thought.

When Katie got back, she said, "Ready?"

"As I'll ever be," I said.

She slid white ankle socks over her evenly tanned, high-arched feet, and then laced up purple and orange-neon running sneakers. I helped her get her backpack on, and we walked toward the trail. The early-morning sun diffused its rays on thinned-out streaks of clouds skittered across the sky above the green treetops, yellow and red and jagged.

3.

Load-Out

I changed quickly into my travel clothes—black skinny tie, charcoal grey suit, dusty black penny loafers—and sauntered out of the visitors' clubhouse toward our team bus, which was parked about forty feet behind the chain-link backstop. There, I leaned on the side of the promotionally-wrapped bus displaying my enormous, grimacing, pitch-delivering face. (I wasn't okay with my image being plastered on it, but Coach Hicks insisted it'd be an effective recruiting tool, so I agreed.) My girlfriend, Shannon Hestian, was waiting for me in her red BMW in the parking lot, but I didn't want to leave just yet.

The air smelled faintly of grass and dirt as I watched the Cortland grounds crew tear down the ball field. The echoes of their manual labor sounded good to me, solid in a way that had the weight of finality to it: baseballs collected into fading-white ball bags, bases lifted from their metal pans; coiled-up hoses, mat-drags, brooms, pounders, and other equipment loaded onto the back of a flat-bed. A blue tarp was waiting to be rolled out, ready to be secured to the ground with cinder blocks to protect the diamond. (Our school's Administration thought it helped to build character for players to prepare and break down the field. Cortland's Administration thought otherwise.)

I had that dragged-out feeling you get after intense physical activity, a calm and quiet feeling, like there's nothing left inside. It's the same kind of feeling you get when you take, say, the 2 line down from the Bronx and ride it all the way down to Grand Central and get your ticket for the Metro-North to Connecticut, for example, and after you're done with all that, you walk out onto the platform for your train and you finally find your own seat, collapsing down blissfully into it.

I heard the crunch of Semzy's Hush Puppies in the gravelly dirt before I saw him. "Enzo, why you do this to yourself?" he said. "It don't help nothin'."

"It's never gonna happen," I said. "Every time, every damn *time* we come this close to beating these guys, somehow we come up short."

"You can't let this shit get to you, man," Semzy said. "Same ol' Cortland. Another conference championship. So what?"

"Sometimes you get tired of being second all the time." I turned and looked at Semzy. Facially, he looked like a college-aged Buck O'Neil. His blue and orange tie in the middle of a navy-blue suit matched our uniform colors. Since he was my catcher, I naturally took everything he said as gospel, pretty much.

The lines of worry on Semzy's brow deepened, like a man unsure of if he ran onto the right train or not as the doors closed. "Losing? Baseball's just for fun, dude. Don't be so serious." I wasn't sure if he meant the game we had just lost, 1-0, or the past seasons' lot of big-game losses. In a way, it didn't matter because losing is cumulative.

"The way things are now," I said, shaking my head, "I feel like all I *can* be is serious. That's the thing about being *really* bad, like when we were freshmen. There's no pressure. But now? Now, it's different." I smoothed out some dirt with my penny loafer, trying to decide whether I should tell Semzy about the secret Shannon had hidden in her belly.

Semzy shook his head with nostalgia in his eyes. "Freshman year. Hey, remember that Zeta party freshman year where they played nothing but Jackson Browne tunes? One of the best parties, ever."

"The night Dickie Briganza puked on Francine Glassbrenner?"

"They played that song *The Load-Out* on loop for like two hours," Semzy said. "No one knew why."

I said, "Y'know, that night was the first time I ever saw Shannon Hestian. Man. Yeah, I remember that night. Things were so different then."

"Lookin' at these dudes," he said, nodding toward the grounds crew, "kinda reminds me of that song." Semzy leaned on the bus, the top of his shoulder touching my enlarged, bus-wrap chin. He folded his arms against his stomach. "The end of things, when you just wanna keep playing."

"Must be nice to have these guys," I said. "Maybe the Cortland athletes can just focus on playing more. 'Stead of worrying about prepping the field and stuff."

Semzy's head recoiled a bit, as if smelling unexpected cigarette smoke. "Maybe. But I like doing the field. It's kinda cool. It's kinda like one o' those things that seems bad, but it's actually not so terrible. Besides, you knew that was the deal when you came to New Paltz. You came here for a reason, right?"

"Yeah," I said, "but I didn't know my arm strength'd keep getting stronger. I didn't know my ligament would snap. I didn't know *any*thing. I just wanted to have fun. But now? Fuck. Now everything's getting so...I don't know. It's weird having to make all these life-changing decisions all of a sudden. It all feels heavy, somehow."

"Remember being in the gym that time, when the whole softball team was running laps around the gym and you were throwing hard for the first time, popping my mitt? Loud-ass echoes, damn." He shook his head at the remembrance of how loud those echoes were.

I said, "Remember Shannon almost tripping over her sneakers trying to tell me to call her?"

"Yeah, she knew right then, dawg. She knew you had it back," Semzy said. "She knew it was time to get her M.R.S."

I just smiled, shaking my head, feeling twin pangs of sadness and nostalgic joy. My head began to ache in pulses.

Semzy said, "Maybe you could let the guys know what you're gonna do next year." He had a serious look on his face, the kind he used with me when he wanted to seem paternal and wise.

"I'm not..." I said, flipping my hands out of my pockets, feeling torn. "I dunno. *I* don't even know what I'm gonna do next year. I haven't even told Shannon yet." I folded my arms against my stomach. "God."

Semzy's eyes narrowed. He seemed to be trying to decide how hard to push the issue. "Remember how fat you got after you got hurt, how different you looked with all that weight on?"

"Remember the beard?" I said.

Semzy said, "Ooh, that was a difficult period in New Paltz College history."

We laughed the laugh of life-long friends reminiscing about the glory days in some road-side bar. It felt good and natural, the kind of laughter that makes you feel like you're at home, right where you're supposed to be. I shoved my hands back into my pants pockets. I said, "Semz, I think we both knew if the surgery held up okay, if everything came back, I'd have to make a decision. One of the Cortland coaches, he told me he was working the gun and I was toppin' out at ninety-two today. And we both know Cortland always has scouts at their games."

"Is this one o' those bromance break-ups?" Semzy said. "That what you're trying to tell me?" His face looked sad to me, resigned to accepting an unavoidable, regrettable fate.

"You know what I mean," I said.

"You could go over there, yeah. And be all serious. And maybe get drafted in the two-hundredth round. Then what?" Semzy said. "You stay here, you're B.M.O.C. And get *all* the spoils, baby."

I couldn't think of anything to say. I looked out at the field. The grounds crew was setting the cinder blocks on the blue tarp now, the final bit of work to be done on the field before it would be left alone in the coming darkness. The sky was a dusky mix of blue, orange, white, and red. Wind blew and rattled through the empty, metallic stands, making me think about all the drunken, full-throated boos and cheers of the Cortland fans, with their faces painted various combinations of red and white. That kind of passion for an NCAA Division-3 baseball team was unusual, exciting. Our fans, when they showed at all, were far more subdued, far more likely to be stoned and silent than drunk and jubilant.

"Prinziatta, I really think you need to think about this," Semzy said. "It ain't like you're some damn first-rounder. You ain't gettin' no million-dollar bonus."

I shuffled at the gravel with my black penny loafers, as if smoothing out infield dirt. I felt a pulling feeling, a yearning for the season not to be over. Not yet, when there was still so much potential left.

Semzy said, "All the guys, they saw you talking to Coach Woodinger after the game. They, we, everyone knows you're back. Back to what you were supposed to be, or whatever. Everybody in that locker room's thinking the exact same thing."

"Yeah?" I said.

"They're thinkin' you gonna be a Mustang next year," said Semzy.

I looked at the ground, squinting my eyes, trying to hide the pain. "Semzy, do you know if girls say they're pregnant a lot, kind of, when they're not, like, pregnant really?" I said.

"That happens," Semzy said. "Occasionally. Shannon?" His eyes told me he sympathized with my position. His eyes also said he knew that such things happened much more than occasionally.

"She just told me," I said. "Yesterday, she told me. In the d-fac line, with everyone standing there and stuff. She's in the car now."

"She gonna transfer, too?" Semzy said. "If you go?"

"Probably," I said. "I don't know. Nothing's for sure, yet. But she wants me to. She thinks if I get drafted, we'll be financially secure. She *thinks* she knows more than she really knows."

"Prinzy, you really oughta think about whether missing out on the most fun year ever is really worth it, just to bum around small-town America for three years, playin' with the Charleston Choo Choos or whatever," Semzy said. "Then you get released and you're working at Enterprise Rental Car for the rest of your life. Listen. We been through a lot together these past few years. It ain't right to just abandon things, just cuz. What kinda life is that? Huh? What kinda life is that?"

I thought about all the good times Semzy and I and our teammates had. I thought about how amazing it would be to walk around campus as the big-time sports star, destined for great things in life while most kids are scrambling to figure out how they'll get by and pay back their loans. I thought about the hallway in McArdle Theater that connected the two exits to the building and how so many theater majors flirted with me there, with the sunshine pouring in from the glass doors on both sides, and the smell of buttery popcorn wafting through the air. I thought about running into Laura Feuntes or Tosha Boydens or Jenny Hillton or Stephie Sugurea, all female sports stars on campus, and how we'd be able to swap stories about winning big games against the toughest odds, and how I'd invite them to grab some Starbucks and share caffeinated laughs and a rare intimacy about the burdens of carrying a team and a student body of fans on your young back. I thought about some of the hippest young professors welcoming me into their inner circle at The Gilded Caravan Wine Bar while they sipped divine vintages, batted philosophy back and forth, and practiced polyamory. All of these visions mixed in my mind like an abstract expressionist painting and I felt my eyes begin to tear up.

Before any lasting damage could be done, I stepped over a watery puddle of beer, and walked past the team bus. I kept walking, head down, hands in my front pockets, toward Shannon's shiny red Beamer.

4.

Fighting Chaos

Josh and Ed passed out as soon as we got back. It was pretty late—the black-and-white yin-yang clock on Ed and Sophia's living room wall pointed to sixteen minutes past oh four hundred hours. Sophia, Ed's wife, liked to look after me. My shoulder was still aching, but the whiskey was helping with the pain. It had been a long night, and yet in a way it was just beginning.

Corporal Ed Horndecker and Private First Class Joshua Neeblin, they've been my buddies since Basic, really, and on through M.O.S. training, Airborne school, and our permanent-duty station assignment down here at Fort Bragg. We're redlegs, artillerymen. We shoot the big guns. I was probably the most unusual paratrooper Sophia had ever known, and that was a part of the bond we shared. I was a little more intellectual than the rest of the guys, and all that meant, practically, was that I got put in the Harley more often, punished with push-ups or sit-ups for my "fancy-ass words." Sophia found me intriguing, I believe. But I'm not really sure.

Sophia said, "So what was really going on tonight?" Her voice still retained some of that aggressive, harsh-edged Bostonian accent, as if every word she said had been bitten off, hard. It wasn't a turn-off, but it almost was.

"Just the usual," I said. "Routine mission gone bad. FUBAR as per usual." I sipped my Jack Daniels.

"The usual FUBAR?" she said. "The usual doesn't end up with a wicked-bad wound to the shoulder." Her halter-top showed off her tan-brown, shiny shoulder. Bringing her pajama-bottomed knees up to her chest, her pink-nailed feet landed on the couch. She wrapped her arms around her legs, as if she were fending off the Massachusetts cold.

"You obviously don't go to these stab-and-jabs much," I said. "They're no joke."

"Dante," she said, scolding me the way she did, with a *wicked* combination of voice tone and condemning eyes. She wiggled her nose, from which gleamed a tiny nose stud made of some kind of blue gem stone.

So, I relented and told her the whole adrenalized story of the chaotic evening.

The September night air smelled faintly of damp pine, chilly and clean, after a few days of rumbling thunderstorms. Anything seemed possible. We pulled into the only empty spot in the lot of the strip mall on All-American Parkway. Stepping out of Ed's flat-bed, the lights from the parking lot and the signs of the stores in the strip mall combined to give off the spooky aura of a movie-set back alley, foreboding and full of shadowy trouble. Streaky puddles of rainwater and gasoline snaked toward lower ground, leaving reflected green, blue, and white rainbows in their paths.

"Dude, man," Josh said. "I'm surprised you made it out with us tonight. The way you were huffing and puffing on that last push-up, bro, I didn't think you had it in you."

"Yeah, man, you need to hit the iron, Dante baby," Ed chimed in. "Hard." He always liked to wear a too-tight, blue polo with an 82nd Airborne Division "AA" patch on the left pec so that everyone could check out his puffy muscles. He was married, happily allegedly, to Sophia, so I'm not sure why it was so important for him to peacock his pecs. "Don't worry, though. We *can* rebuild you!"

Ed and Josh fist-bumped, smiling. In different ways, they were better soldiers than me, but we got along in spite of that. Usually in the Army, I'd noticed, like hung with like. The high-speed/low-drag guys hung together and the "broke dicks" hung together. I was a broke dick because I had fractured my fibula on a jump in Cuba ten months prior. I was working my way back to high-speed/low-drag status.

"Mark Twain said he never did any exercising except for sleeping and resting. That's good advice," I said. "And Douglas Adams died running on a treadmill. But no, it's better to spend all my jump pay on Creatine and steroids and pump iron 'til my heart explodes, like you two meatheads."

Three girls, one blonde and two brunettes, emerged from behind blue dumpsters, walking toward their car as we were walking toward the bar. When we were even with them, Josh, in a cream-colored shirt with black buttons, jeans, and cowboy boots, started walking backward, right in step with their pacing. Once they figured what he was doing, they laughed and then we laughed, too. "G'night, ladies!" Josh said, putting on the brakes. "You're leaving too early, I'm telling ya. Party's gonna be inside, not out here!" He turned and started jogging to catch up with us.

As we entered The Boot Scoot, The Drive-By Truckers' classic "The Three Great Alabama Icons" played overhead, guitars blazing. The lighting was dim. Black-leather swivel chairs lining the long bar had scratch marks all along their black-painted, iron legs. The wood floor was faded-tan to almost-white in some places, also scratched up to the point where you felt bad, almost, for walking on it. A huge banner hung over the space where bands played, displaying a giant piano keyboard floating over a blue ocean, an orange sun setting, and palm trees all around, punctuated by random black musical notes. A small pink balloon, almost deflated, rested by one of the legs of a bar chair near the back exit. We sat down and ordered three bottles of Bud.

Sitting at the bar, my mind flashed back to the time Josh got us kicked out of a hotel bar because he wouldn't stop talking in a Russian accent and demanding the bartender make him a "real" White Russian. And the time Ed accidentally locked us out of his truck, and I had to forage a coat hanger from a dumpster so overflowing with fish heads and other stinky food scraps we had to drive all the wintery way home with the windows open and the smell was still so bad that Josh up-chucked out the window three times along the way. And the time Josh went missing for two hours and came back saying he met the most incredible girl, and he was in love, and he finally had found his soulmate, only to discover, later, that she was actually a transvestite.

At the vague peripheral image of women's hair flowing into the bar, we looked over and saw the three girls Josh walked with entering the bar. The blonde with a pink barrette in her hair looked pissed, her features crunched into a "no approach" bitch-face. The other two, though, had open, excited looks on their faces. As they walked past us, the brunette with deep dimples said, lightly, invitingly, "Hey-ey."

They came back! "The wonderful magic of Joshua Neeblin," I thought. "He can sell ice cubes to an Eskimo, that kid. If the term "ladies' man" hadn't been co-opted by a bad comedy film, that's what I'd call him."

The three girls sat at a table toward the back of the place, then the blonde quickly got up and went to the bar to order a drink. That was all the sign Josh and I needed.

I noticed, first, on the one I liked, her dimples. They were hard not to notice—definitely in the same realm as a Jennifer Garner or Leighton Meester, the kind of unusual facial feature that almost always drew my eye. Living in a world of olive-drab conformity made my brain seek out colorful outliers anywhere, it seemed.

"Now we're gonna play a little game, okay?" Josh said, as we sat down at their table.

"Sure!"

Josh said, "What're your names?"

"Ashlynne."

"Donnatella."

"So, lemme ask you guys something, because it's very strange, and we, I dunno," said Josh. "We kinda don't know what to make of it."

"Okay?" said Donnatella. Her face, thin but with bulbous cheek bones, told a story of being intrigued and loving the feeling of mystery coming over her at this moment.

"Well, our buddy over there at the bar, his name is Ed, okay?" Josh said.

"Okay," said Donnatella.

"And when he was dating his wife, like, the second or third date they went on, something like that, after the date was over, Ed came back to his place, and he found this ring with a little, like, scroll in it and two little blue feathers around it. He was cleaning and he found it underneath his sofa cushions."

"Really?" Ashlynne said.

"Yeah, and so what he does is, he goes down to this, like, I dunno what you call it, this, like, store that sells, like...."

"An occult store?" said Donnatella.

"Yeah!" said Josh. "Exactly, see, you know what I'm talking about! And anyway, this store, they claim to sell stuff like dragon's blood and crap like that. And Ed took the ring there and the scroll and the feathers and asked them if they could make any sense out of it."

"Ooooh," said Ashlynne. "What did they say?"

"Well, they told him that actually, the ring and the scroll and the feathers were like this crazy ancient love spell."

"Really?!"

"Yeah, and..."

I looked over at Ed at the bar. "Triangle Formation," I thought. I quick-whistled at Josh, and tapped my nose three times with my left index finger. We both stood up.

"Excuse us, ladies," Josh said. "You guys might wanna head to the back of the bar. Seriously. Something bad is about to go down, and I am not kidding."

We walked, slowly, toward the bar. There was a white guy with a blond Mr. Kotter afro and a dyckman, wearing a black leather jacket, talking too excitedly to Candy, the town old-lady wino. He seemed to be on some kind of uppers, meth most likely, and based on what he was saying, rapid-fire, he seemed to think Candy should provide him some money due to the fact that he needed it, and that he would pay her back at some unspecified point in the future.

I walked directly toward him while Josh walked casually around toward the front entrance, so that he would be approaching from the rear. I signaled to Ed, who nodded and stayed in position, ready to pounce when the Triangle Formation called for it.

Faux-drunkenly I said, "Heyyy Big Man, why don't you just go to the ATM across the street? Everybody got money in an ATM! Ain't you got no money, pussy boy?"

Predictably, he swung the knife I knew he was hiding in his right hand inside his jacket pocket at me, catching me on the right shoulder. Josh, a few seconds later than the Triangle Formation plan called for, tackled him from behind, joined in tandem by Ed.

Someone then tackled me, and I must have struck my head because I blacked out. I woke up in the hospital, and then Sophia was there with the guys and we all drove back to Ed and Sophia's house.

"So that's what happened, basically," I said. "Try to do something nice, take a knife to the shoulder."

"So what happened with the girls?" Sophia said. "Are you gonna try to find them somehow, facebook or something?"

"We'll run into them again," I said. "Or not. It doesn't really matter."

"I just don't know what to do with you, Dante," Sophia said.

"Shouldn't you be heading off to bed or something?" I said. "The guys were cooked. But you know my tolerance. If you try to keep up with me, you'll get alcohol poisoning."

Sophia picked up a book off the coffee table that I had left there after a party about a week earlier. It was a book of poems by Charles Bukowski. She folded herself into herself sitting next to me on the couch. Her raven-black hair and dark brown eyes were hidden beneath a beat-up Red Sox cap. "Why did you bring this book to the party last week?"

"Isn't it obvious?"

"No," she said, "that's why I'm asking, dum-dum."

"I wanted to class up your little shin-dig. That's all," I said. "I dunno what kind of riff-raff you're gonna be having at these things."

"Class it up?" she said. "With *this*?" She held the book up to her crinkled nose, as if smelling feces.

"Mister Charles Bukowski is a very respected man of letters, I'll have you know, young lady."

"Hard to believe," she said.

"Maybe so," I said. "But Jackson Pollack is also considered to be high art. Bukowski brings poetic language to and from the gutters."

"You're so smart, Dante. You know that?" Sophia said.

"He's the patron saint of alcoholics, drug addicts, and derelicts the world over."

"You get a little philosophical when you drink, you know that?" Sophia said.

"Could be worse."

"Yah," I said.

Sophia said, "So, philosopher-man, why? Why are you boys living this way?"

I said, "What way?"

"I mean, don't you have any morals or what?"

"You know what Nietzsche says about morals," I said.

Sophia said, "Nietzsche's dead, so if he says anything at all I'd call that a miracle."

"Nietzsche says—nice try, by the way—Nietzsche says that morality is simply slavery to custom. That's all it is," I said. "Isn't that great? Isn't that just terrific? I was reading that last week, and I thought, 'Man! Yes. That's so right!' Amazing stuff. Terrible name, but amazing philosopher."

"You just love to read don't you?" Sophia said.

I said, "Only books."

"Uh-huh," she said. "You're such, like, an odd bird, Dante. What the hell am I gonna do with you?"

"And not only that, but get this, get this! *Any* ol' custom will do. Those who follow the custom are called moral, those who don't immoral," I said. "Even if the custom is throwing virgins into a volcano. Doesn't matter. *Any* custom will do."

"So, what's your moral philosophy, then? Because something tells me this is leading up to Dante Kronos's brilliant new moral philosophy to bestow upon the eagerly awaiting world," she said, grinning all coy and cute.

I said, "One word—joy."

"Joy? That's a little thin to make a manifesto out of," she said. "Usually these things have to be blog-post length at least, these days."

"Joy, Sophia, joy! Do what makes you happy. It's simple, and that's what makes it so good."

She said, "So what happens when your joy runs up against the law? Or someone else's joy? Huh? What then, Joy-Boy?"

"Well, then you have to make a risk management decision."

"Risk management? For a joy-hound?" Sophia said.

"Yes, because going to prison is the ultimate killjoy."

"I don't think I can get on board with this."

"Why not?" I said.

She said, "Cuz it's crazy, obviously."

I said, "You mean, because you were raised Roman Catholic. A religious framework or worldview, like, that rewards guilt, shame, monotheism, and monogamy. You haven't been trained to be open to new philosophies. You've been trained to see things a certain way, and so you do."

"Ah, the rub. Finally," she said.

"Your belief system is auto-filtering the goodness of this thing," I said. "Can't you see that?"

"How's that?" she said.

"It works on a subconscious level. You don't even really know it's happening. That's kinda like the beauty of it."

She said, "And so from this, then, I can expect you to say polyamory among adults, drug legalization, prostitution, and an unlimited number of firearms up to and including a nuclear weapons are all okey-dokey for Mr. Joy-Boy?"

"Yes, yes, yes, and hell yes!" I said. "Now you're starting to see how this works. It's a beautiful thing, really."

"I'm sorry, but I'm really not buying this." Sophia got up and plucked another beer from the refrigerator. She came and sat back down.

"You know what's weird?" I said. I sipped some whiskey. It burned, but I enjoyed the burning.

"You?"

"I've had *Ride of the Valkyries* stuck in my head all week," I said.

"That is weird. Why do you think that is?" she said. She didn't open the beer. She just slid it onto the coffee table.

"I don't know. It's a nice tune," I said.

"It is," she said.

"My sister Hebbe used to play it in her room on loop on DVD all the time. God knows why," I said. "Probably rebelling against pop culture and New Kids on the Block or something."

"Don't hate on Marky Mark," Sophia said.

"Have I....Did I ever....Do you know what happened with my sister Hebbe?"

"You mentioned her once when you were in a drunken stupor," Sophia said. "I couldn't really understand what you were saying, though. Something about bison, it sounded like."

I said, "Myyyy sister Hebbe when she was sixteen years old was on a subway car headed uptown, on her way to school, at about seven A.M. The car was crowded, as they tend to be at that hour of a New York City commuting workday. And a grad student who worked at a bio lab at CCNY, who had *no* authorization to be carrying around samples in public, but despite this was carrying around, for Zeus only knows what reason, a vial full of ricin..."

"Oh God," said Sophia, covering her mouth with her hands.

"Not bison. So this complete moron, he's fumbling around with his bagel and his coffee—this is all from what we were told by the police and everybody, we don't know for sure—and somehow, the vial falls out of his bag. You can imagine the reaction once people realized there was some kind of particulate in the air, and it affected everyone's breathing and everything."

"Oh my God, Dante, I'm so sorry."

"Yeah," I said. "The really good news was that out of all the people on the car, only three died. One being my sister Hebbe. On account of her asthma and what the medical people like to call a weakened immune system but what I like to call not being in very good shape. *And* just random bullshit. Random bullshit like proximity to the toxin versus proximity to the door, distance to the next stop, the ability of the medical people to get to her in a crowded and hectic underground environment and get her to a hospital on time to save her and about eight thousand other completely random factors that could never be accounted for, even if you tried."

"Oh my God. That's awful, just awful," Sophia said. Her eyes were tearing up.

"Sophia, I will have you know that I am a United States paratrooper with the God-damned Eighty-Second Airborne Division. And even if I were the fucking Commander-in-Chief and the Eighty-Second reported *to* me..."

"Yes," she said, unsteadily.

"And still....I would have no power to change the chaotic nature and the complete randomness of the universe."

Sophia sat there for a moment, tears in her eyes, thinking in that beautiful way that she sat thinking, with her eyes turned up and to the left, her philtrum quivering. Finally, she said, "And all of this, then, to say that the world is, like, just all this random chaos so why not enjoy the brief flicker of time we have on it? Throw out custom, throw out religion, and so long as we're not hurting anyone, then just do whatever the hell makes us happy in the moment. Right? Is that it?"

"You're God-damn right."

Sophia unfolded herself on the couch, and moved closer to me. We looked at each other guiltily for a moment, then moved toward each other, our lips nearly meeting in a hungry kiss. "No!" she said, in a child-like voice, as if scolding a puppy. She pulled away. "I'm. I'm sorry," she said. "But I..." Her voice trailed off, then she stood up, and walked out of the room.

I sat there for some indecipherable amount of time, feeling sad, and hearing *Ride of the Valkyries* over and over in my head. I got up, at some point—I don't know when—and headed for the latrine. In the hallway, I looked into Ed and Sophia's bedroom. Sophia was on top of the cobalt-blue comforter, huddled in right close to snoring Ed, clutching Lee-Lee, her all-time favorite one-eyed teddy bear.

5.

Storytime

Hey, you're new here, right? Wanna hear a story? Okay, so picture this, picture this. Two male voices, one deep and one less so, over black.

"No."

"Why not?"

"Because it's stupid."

"Which part?"

"The whole thing."

"Aw, come on."

"It doesn't make sense economically, realistically, creatively, or any other way. Other than that, it's perfect."

"You're just being negative."

"No, dude, I'm trying to save you a bunch of time and money. Forget it. Look, I gotta go. My Maybach is in a loading zone, and Natalia, this Venezuelan model I'm seeing, is probably eating all the caviar already. I'll see ya on Monday."

My mind clicks, sometimes, when people tell me no, and then all of a sudden, I start thinking about all of the ways I could kill, for example, deep-voiced Bill d'Magia and get away with it. Kill his Venezuelan model girlfriend, kill his caviar, kill his stupid Maybach. I start thinking about wanting to kill his entire family, every friend he ever had, everyone who ever said more than "Good morning" to him in his life. I think about doing it slow, with a samurai sword, so I could make that guy bleed. I think about slicing every inch of his perfectly-tanned skin off his body, to make sure he never ever reproduced, so that the plague of his bloodline would be wiped off the face of the Earth forever. But don't worry. Those're just passing thoughts, not anything real. I'd never hurt anyone, especially not big Billy.

That was a conversation I had, anyways, word for word with the legend that is Bill d' Magia. He's a guy I work with here at Oculent Financial. He's a sales guy, an alpha male, always hitting on random women and flying to Vegas where his room is comped and his champagne is always chilled and ready to go. And he is *good* at his job. He totally kills it every day. I don't know how he does it. But he does. And *that's* why I was talking to him about my idea. It's a *great* idea, an incredible idea. Bill didn't think so. Bill can't see it yet. But that's the way it is for all really big new ideas. People can't see 'em for anything. They can't look out into the future and see anything different than their own current (and usually boring as all get-out) lives. But that's my problem, not yours. You were wanting to hear about my idea, because you're particularly intelligent.

Have you ever heard of a social object? No? Here, take a quick look at the Wikipedia page here on my phone: "Social objects are objects around which social networks form. The concept was put forward by Jyri Engeström in 2005 as part of the explanation of why some social networks succeed and some fail. Engeström maintained that: "Social network theory fails to recognise such real-world dynamics because its notion of sociality is limited to just people." Instead, he proposed what he called "object centered sociality," citing the work of the sociologist Karin Knorr-Cetina. For example, Engeström maintained that much of the success of the popular photo-sharing site Flickr was due to the fact that photographs serve as social objects around which conversations of social networks form. The concept was popularized by Hugh MacLeod, cartoonist and social observer, in 2007."

Well, I want to create a social object around literature, for people who like *books*. Yeah, I work in the financial services industry, but my true passion is literature. I was an English Lit major back in school, and I've always wanted to share this passion with as many people as possible. And *that's* what this idea was, to get that going. But Bill just rejected it, right out of hand.

He didn't even give me a chance to *really* explain the idea, all of the nuances and the deeper explanations about how everything would work. And trust me, it'll work. It'll work just like magic.

But anyway, yeah. Right over here.

Welcome, my friend, to cubicle number 612-C, in the heart of the sixth floor of the Ring Lardner, Senior building in beautiful Austin, Texas! Yes! We're working in the epicenter of Oculent Financial Corporation, one of the most exciting companies in all of America. Here in cubicle number 612-C, we've got everything you could ever want or ask for. We got a computer, including not one but two monitors! and a mouse (*with* a mouse pad!) And a keyboard. Other very fine amenities of this here cubicle include a stapler! A staple remover! A scotch tape dispenser! A telephone! Binder clips! Paper clips! Small spiral notebooks! A calculator! Files! And reference books! Lots and lots of financial regulations reference books! We do a *lot* of research here at Oculent Financial, trying to stay ahead of the market and see the trends of tomorrow today.

Me? What do I do here at Oculent Financial? That's a great question. I do *some* research, yeah. Gotta know the market and the terminology—the vocabulary—of this particular field. *Then* what I do is I hop on the phone, and I comm*un*icate, man. I communicate with as many people as possible. And it's my job to "tee up" the sale. We're trying to get people to be more financially secure for their future, for their golden years. So, y'know, there's, like, four-hundred million people in America! And we really want everyone to take control of their financial future by letting us manage their portfolio. So, I communicate with 'em and determine if it sounds like they're serious about their financial future. And then if they are, I hand 'em off to Bill, or some of our other heavy hitters like Bill. They make the sales. I just kind of help 'em out.

Which is why, or one of the reasons why, Bill should totally help *me* out with my idea. I help his ass every day, and he makes mad commissions off my leads. He wouldn't even have his Maybach lifestyle if it weren't for me, and other people like me here at Oculent. And here he is saying no. What a crock.

Ever notice how no one helps out anymore? Used to, people would help each other out. But now? Thing's have changed. You could stumble around this god-damned planet like some stumblebum drunk ruining everyone's night by pissing in a corner of the world with a lamp shade on your head, and still, no one would think to try and help you out any. That's the problem with this whole Universe. It's an uncaring, unfeeling place that no one is even paying any god-damned attention to, anyway. So, why should it matter? Why does it matter? But, see, *that's* why my idea is so good. It's gonna bring people together and make the world a *much* better place. I just need some capital and some coaching from someone like Bill, and I can really make it take off. I'll be good to go then, really. It's gonna be fantastic, trust me.

But what Bill doesn't know is I've got a plan. I've got a helluva plan to get him on board. And when you think about it, it's quite obvious that the plan will work simply because it is brilliant and magnificent. That's really all there is to it. Why don't you meet me at my house tonight, and maybe we can talk more about my idea over a cold brewski? Sound good? Yeah, I got frosted mugs and everything at my place. It'll be awesome. I even got a pretty good sandwich bar I can put together. It'll be super-awesome, yeah. Trust me. Sliced onions and everything.

Welcome to my humble abode! This is my weekend cubicle, if you will. Yeah, it's weird that it's number 612 also, but that's the only one they had unoccupied when I came here. Nothing I could really do about that.

Yeah, yeah, watch your step, watch your step. I got a few cats running around here. There's Raymond and Carve and Fordster and Pussy Hemingway and a bunch of others. They're all strays that I picked up along the way. They come to me all starving and whatnot, and I feed 'em up. Then I try to give 'em a safe place to stay and hang out till they're back in good spirits again. And then I try to find a good, solid permanent home for 'em. You'd be surprised how many good people are looking for a cat as a pet. Not enough social objects in their lives, I guess. But whatever, at least I know I'm bringing some value into their lives.

Yeah, I know... that smell, right? It's a bit overpowering at first. But don't worry. You get used to it. You really do. After a while, you won't even notice it, I promise. It's something that doesn't even register for me—like, at all. I'm used to it now.

I've never understood people who don't love their pets. I mean, pets can really help you cope with all of the bad stuff life throws at you. It's the pets who know how to give unconditional love, not the stupid humans. The humans don't come close to understanding trust or unconditional love or anything even approaching kindness or compassion. It's almost like pets are better than humans because with pets, at least you know where you stand. With humans, damn if I know what they're thinking at any given time. Some girl gives you her number in a bar after you're making out with her for like a half an hour, and then you call her the next day, and it's some anarchist bookstore in Dripping Springs. What the heck is that? What. Is. That? A pet would never screw you over like that!

You want a beer? Yeah, of course. Here. A nice head on that guy. Mug is cold as heck. Hey, let's sit down in the living room. Careful, watch your hand. It's really cold.

I don't know if you've ever heard of this software? It's called Prezi? And it's pretty cool. It's like a cooler version of PowerPoint, for the hipster crowd. You probably don't like having to learn new software—who does?—but this thing's pretty amazing because you can put together a presentation that *isn't* boring as *heck*—I know! Amazing, right? All bow down to the digital altar of Prezi!

Well, I figured I'd do a demo, or a beta test. A run-through. See if it'd look like what I thought it would. Cuz I'm planning to use it for my social object idea. To kind of spice things up. So, I set up one of those flip-camera things in the bike room here, set up the presentation to project onto the wall, dimmed the lights, and let her rip.

Now, this event is called....ready? Ready to have your mind blown? It's called "Fine Wine and Once Upon a Time!" Awesome, right? And what happens is, when people come in, we have some wine available for them. And so they grab some wine and take a seat or whatever.

Now, the first Prezi "slide" they see shows a quote from Robert Bly's great book, "Iron John: A Book About Men." It says, "The knowledge of how to build a nest in a bare tree, how to fly to the wintering place, how to perform the mating dance—all of this information is stored in the reservoirs of the bird's instinctual brain. But human beings, sensing how much flexibility they might need in meeting new situations, decided to store this sort of knowledge outside the instinctual system; they stored it *in stories*. Stories, then, amount to a reservoir where we keep new ways of responding that we can adopt when the conventional and current ways wear out."

That shows on the screen up there. Then I say something like, I go: So, stories then, traditionally as we humans continually evolved throughout history, served a distinct and useful purpose. They gave us direction and kept us from falling too far off track. Now, in modern storytelling, we've gotten to this point called postmodernism. And postmodernism pokes fun at this notion. The basic idea is that since science is kind of proving that there really is no objective truth anyway, writing stories that serve to tell some moralistic truth is absurd. Now, I could get into the reasons for why there is no objective truth, but it's very philosophical and is probably of interest only to academics and philosophers with syphilis and hard-to-spell names like Friedrich Nietzsche and Immanuel Kant anyway. So, who here thinks stories should have a message? Some hands go up, right? And who here thinks stories shouldn't have a message? And some more hands go up, or whatever.

Well, if stories *shouldn't* have a message, what should they have? What could be their purpose? That's Lecture Two in this series. So, stay tuned for that. And just kind of mull that over, some food for thought, as you listen to this next thing. Because what happens next is I play an audiobook version of a fairy tale called "Iron John." And, see, what I'm saying now to you is what I'll say to the crowd. I'll be like, this story definitely *does* have a message. It was written a long time ago, and based on oral traditions even older than that. The Brothers Grimm walked the

Earth from 1785 to 1863 in Germany, so as the world started to become enlightened, so to speak, they started writing down all of these oral traditions, or folklore tales, if you will. This particular version you are about to hear is the Robert Bly translation of the Brothers Grimm tale, as narrated by yours truly. Now, one thing you *could* do while you listen, if you have a drink, you *could* drink every time the number *three* is mentioned. There will be a little bell afterward. Now, you are *only* allowed to do this if you *will not* be driving home after this. So, only if you have a designated driver or if you plan on sleeping here over night. So, without further adieu, ladies and gentlemen, I give you "Iron John" by the Brothers Grimm.

And then I play the audio, and while the audio is playing, some images pop up on the screen to sort of coincide with the story, and to give people something to focus their eyes on while the audio plays. The story is about forty minutes long or so. Thereabouts.

Then after that, we have a Question and Answer session where I ask for questions from the audience and stuff. Sooo, what do you think? Still not convinced? Well, I'm gonna show Bill the video tomorrow, see what he thinks. He's gonna love it, man. You'll see. You'll see. It's gonna be magic. He's gonna back me, a hundred percent, and then I'll have my start-up money, and eventually I'll be bought out by venture capitalists for three hundred million dollars and I'll go lie on a beach somewhere with three supermodels catering to my every whim. No, really.

Why are you laughing?

So, anyway, I finally got big Bill to agree to take a look at the video, as a kind of demo, like, of what it *would* look like when it went live. He was eating a pastrami-on-rye sandwich during the twenty minutes he takes for lunch. He said, a mouth full of sandwich, "No."

"What no?"

"No, the whole thing is wrong, your whole whatchamacallit, the premise. Stories aren't what you, or that other yahoo, Black or whatever..."

anymore. Each time the Lady Hawks ran by Semzy he stood up, and I paused my relationship therapy.

"How much weight'd you lose, Enzo?" Semzy said, as we were leaving.

"About fifty," I said.

"Fifty pounds? Really?"

"Yeah," I said. "More or less."

"And how'd this happen again? When you told me what you were gonna do before I wasn't really paying attention. People usually don't do what they say they're gonna do anyways, so it's more efficient not to pay too much attention."

"Quit drinking beer. Cut out carbs, big-time. No dairy, no gluten."

"That's it?" Semzy said.

"Pretty much," I said. "After the surgery, I kind of slacked off. But now I'm in Beast Mode again. Ha! No one wants to see some Hideki Irabu kind of fat toad trying to pitch."

"Beast Mode, huh?" said Semzy. "What were you in before? Feast Mode?"

We laughed. One of the things I loved about Semzy was that he shared my out-of-fashion enjoyment of puns, even weak ones.

Semzy said, "Well. Beast Mode's paying off. You're bringing it. The mitt's poppin'."

Watching the Lady Hawks running their laps, I started thinking about Jenny. "Jenny Drama" people called her, because she was an actress and also because she was addicted to drama. We'd spent a few months being so completely into each other it felt like there was no way it could ever go wrong, but then, all of a sudden, it did, and it was—apparently—irrecoverable. I said, "Semz, is there any way you know of to save time on figuring out what a girl is *really* like?"

"That's usually what dating is for," said Semzy. "Isn't it?"

"I know, but it just takes so long. And by the time you realize you're not right for each other, you've wasted six months of your life, and your chest hurts every time you think about her."

"Huh," said Semzy. "Jenny Drama?"

I didn't need to acknowledge that this was about her. Everyone on campus would know it was about her, so of course

Semzy knew. I said, "It's just. It's just, like, a matter of efficiency, like you said about listening to people. Y'know, Professor Ferriss says that time, actually, is the only resource..."

"Wait a minute, wait just one minute!" Semzy said. "We could design a sort of a ...I dunno... a series of scenarios where a girl has to make a choice or take some action, and then we rate her performance according to a preference scale..."

"Yeah! *My* preference scale!" I said. "I like, I like. It's action-based. You learn more about people that way, I think."

"Right. And we'd design it so it seems like a bunch of random stuff just kind of happens. Maybe even make some kind of a psych project out of it. Maybe one of the Psych majors can help us design it. Publish something, even. If it goes well."

I said, "Yeah. And we'll get femiNazi bomb packages, too, in the mail every day of our lives!"

"Ha. But maybe how we can sell it as a project is like, what if dating roles were reversed? What if men tested women, instead of vice-versa? What if women had to take the risk of asking men out? Something like that. Like a social experiment type of thing. People love that about colleges, that kind of stuff."

"Yeah! And we can get some grad-student buy-in by expanding out," I said. "Like, mating choices affect marriages, which affect kids and families, which affect communities, and eventually nations, and the world. So, really, mating choices are the whole ballgame!"

Semzy said, "Okay, so who should be our first test subject?"

As we hit the double-doors of the gym's west exit, Shannon Hestian, the last girl in the running line the Lady Hawks had going, made a "call me" gesture at me. Shannon was ranked by *Softball America* as the third best college pitcher in the country. She had also recently appeared, through a veil of sexy smoke on the pitcher's mound wearing a unique uniform, in *ESPN: The Magazine's* "Body Issue."

"I think we have our first volunteer," I said. "Funny how life works."

Semzy said, "You do know every girl on campus is gonna, like, hate us if this ever gets out, right?"

I sighed, melodramatically, "The price you pay for doing good research!" I said.

II.

Later, Semzy told me how the first of our little experiments went down:

"Have you read *Franny and Zooey*?" Semzy said.

"Yeah, I had to read it freshman year for some reason. I forget why," Shannon said.

They were sitting at a study table in the Chiaro Scurro Library, textbooks and notebooks laid open on a scholarly table.

"What'd you think about it?"

"It was okay," Shannon said. "I felt bad for Franny."

"Because of the existential crisis she's going through?"

"Well, no. I mean, yeah, that, too. But more, it's like, no one was even, like, touching her or anything. Like, giving her a hug or anything like that. And Zooey was just this big know-it-all type, kind of. Hell-bound to spout off on his beliefs and everything. I just wanted poor Franny to punch him in the face."

"I see," said Semzy. "You didn't think in the end Zooey saves her from her suffering? Kind of helps her get over her crisis?"

"No, if anything, he just made it worse with all his verbal shenanigans."

Semzy looked down at his script. "Even though at the end it says, 'For joy, apparently, it was all Franny could do to hold the phone, even with both hands,' that kinda thing?" he said. "Doesn't that suggest to you some kind of a psychological breakthrough? Or at least some kind of transformation? Or something like that?"

"Yeah. But so what?" said Shannon. "It's still not a hug. Not one hug in the whole damn story. It was just so sad."

"Hmm. Interesting." On a light blue index card, Semzy wrote, "#FAIL."

III.

For Act Two of our little staged-play, I was watching from about a hundred yards away, through binoculars. Our curly-haired shortstop, Jared Besto, was walking along the same cobblestone path as Shannon, walking toward her. Right when he was passing her, he did a funny version of "LeBronning," flopping to the ground like a fish wriggling on a hook and writhing around in fake pain. I watched Shannon's reaction to this very closely. At first, she recoiled back in shock. (As I would expect.) When it seemed clear that Jared was just clowning, she awkwardly smiled, and started to walk away.

Then the second half of the plan unfolded: Jared, on the ground, shouted, "Ow! I'm hurt! I'm *really* hurt! Ahhh! I *really* hurt myself! I think I sprained my fucking ankle! Someone help! Help me! I think I sprained my ankle! Someone call an ambulance! Please!"

Shannon crinkled her nose, looking somewhat confused at the spectacle before her, shook her blonde hair, and walked away.

On a yellow index card, I wrote, "#FAIL."

IV.

For Act Three, we recruited Heather Heatherington, the one female sports reporter on staff at *The Oracle*, to set up an interview with Shannon. (A hundred bucks and a few beers will get you almost anything on a college campus.) After some "softball" questions about her softball career, Heather got down to the business of asking about me.

"Have you heard the rumors that Enzo Prinziatta's throwing ninety-five miles an hour again?"

"No, I haven't really paid attention to that," Shannon said.

"Really?" Heather said. "I've heard the same thing from several different sources."

Shannon shrugged. "I'm more concerned with my own pitching, I guess."

"There's another rumor going around that you two might be a couple," Heather said. "Any truth to that? You'd make a really cute couple!"

"No," Shannon said. "No truth to that."

Heather then circled back to the upcoming softball season, expectations for the team, and whether Shannon thought she'd accept an invitation to play in the Olympics. Then, one last time: "Y'know, if you and Enzo *were* to be a couple, and if he's throwing heat again to the point where he's a first-round draft pick or something like that, that would be something the media, the mainstream media—not just *The Oracle*—would probably pounce on, maybe. The two of you—the Bombshell and the Bullet? Something like that? And, y'know, that kind of publicity...I mean, people pay a *lot* of money to grab that much media attention. So, is there *any* possibility *whatsoever* you two might get together?"

"Bombshell's a bit much, I think," Shannon said. "But no, I really don't. I mean, I haven't really thought about it. We kind of know each other a little, or whatever, and we're sort of like friends, kinda, but that's about it. I don't want to comment further about this at this time."

After listening to the audio playback on Heather's little digital recorder, I could hear the strain in Shannon's voice in her last answer, the kind of strain that told me she was lying. I wrote on a pink index card, "#FAIL."

V.

We met, Shannon and I, by purely random, magical chance, apparently, in a hallway in the Albert Ellis wing of the Psychology building. I looked at Shannon's Irish-green eyes, enchanting and alive, almost electric in their power, and the kind of fresh nervous-excitement like I got at the outset of a ballgame hit me. It usually struck about the time when the home-plate ump rolled out a brand new, shiny baseball toward the base of the mound, and the ball lay there half-shrouded by grass in all of its potential, waiting, pulsing. Shannon's eyes held, somehow, the promise of revealing millennia-old secrets never before told. Just like that baseball at the base of the mound, they played as the exciting possibility of a passion exhausted on a field of romantic competition. And yet, they were also just a girl's green eyes.

Her philtrum wiggled above her thin upper lip, quivering ever so slightly as she seemed to be trying to look shy and expectant, like a kid vaguely anticipating a new toy as her mother held her hand walking through Kings Plaza. Looking at her, I still had that fluttery kind of feeling like I got walking out to the mound for the first inning of the game, feeling that inner tug of explosive energy, barely contained. This stirring up of buried devotion, the wrangling of my inner wild man hell-bent on releasing the hell-hounds of virility and courage, was for me a pharmacopeia of euphoria. I smiled, raised my left eyebrow, and said, "Hey, Shannon."

The fluorescent indoor light beamed from behind her, giving her hair the luminescent outline of a blonde halo. A round spot of blanched sunshine draining in from the west bay window drenched a portion of Shannon's left leg, in tight black leggings. Pink woolen socks peeked out above the tops of her brown calf-length boots, which had one strap-and-buckle near the top and another one down toward the ankle. A grey, short-sleeve sweater topped a black long-sleeve shirt, and over these Shannon sported a once-wrapped, wide, pink, indoor scarf with tassel-strings hanging off each end.

Shannon said, "Hey, did you know, apparently, there's some rumor going around that, uhh, me and you...kinda like... y'know. That we should, you and I..."

"What?" I said, playing dumb, egging her on. "Just come right out and say what you wanna say. Be empowered!"

"Well, they're saying we should kinda, y'know. Us? Y'know, the softball pitcher and the baseball pitcher?"

"I don't get it, what?" I said. "They want us to throw our bullpens together or something? And who's this they anyways?"

She giggled, tucking her chin underneath her nose and lifting her eyes at me like a wounded kitten.

I said, "So, you're wanting me to ask you out? Is that what you're saying here?"

Shannon placed some blonde hair behind her left ear and shrugged.

7.

Root Cause

November 5, 2014

Maria Forestino, L.L.C.
Attorneys-at-Law
42-42 Livermore Avenue
Brooklyn, NY 12354

Dear Ms. Forestino,

We received the following from our estranged son, Theodore Ardle. Since you represent him, we thought you might want to review it. Frankly, we're just praying that he comes to his senses and complies completely with the authorities.

Please consider the following to determine whether or not it may assist our son's cause. I thank you in advance for your professional diligence.

Sincerely,
Margaret Ardle

DRAFT
Writing Chronicle: Day 1, 3:05 A.M.

Dear Mr. Chairman, Members of the New York State Board of Pardons and Paroles, and Parole Commissioners:

I am writing this letter because if I tried to tell you these things during a parole board hearing, I would break down crying, probably, and you wouldn't have time to listen to the whole thing, since the system is so backed up with pending cases. So, I'm writing it down in the hopes that you might read it in advance of my hearing in order to give it the time and consideration it really deserves.

Some might call it a trick, just a cheap magic trick, but I believe that the best psychologists practicing today will tell you that the environment in which a child grows up plays a pretty big role in the psychological development of that child. I've spoken to several of the state-paid shrinks they send here over the years I've been imprisoned at the beautiful Leonard Alfred Schneider Unit and even they seem to have come to the same conclusion, if somewhat reluctantly. That being the case, I thought you might like to know what *my* childhood was like, since it probably had a significant influence on me and how I turned out, ultimately, and what part it played in the crime I committed against the people of the State of New York. This includes the enragement issues I seem to have, according to the psychological personnel. And I can't entirely disagree.

I am told—and medical records exist to corroborate the story—that I was born with my mother's umbilical cord wrapped around my neck. That was my introduction to life—being choked to death. Imagine the impact this must have had on me. The experts in the field now refer to this as an "epigenetic" impact, which means certain genes inside of me were turned on or off based on environmental stimuli. So, from my very first moment on Earth, I understood (deep down in my D.N.A.) on a genetic and epigenetic level that this world is every-second dangerous. Around every corner, in every creeper's van, on every city block lurked unimaginable horrors waiting to effortlessly extinguish my life. And this wisdom was burned into my subconscious brain without me even knowing it until much, much later and after countless hours of intense, court-ordered therapy. Imagine the consequences of having this kind of wisdom running behind the scenes, controlling *your* every belief, thought, and action. How well-adjusted would *you* be? Would you be on the parole board or seeking parole?

To be technical, my birth was what's called a Type-B nuchal cord birth, which is generally described as a hitch which cannot be undone and ends up as a true knot. (As opposed to Type A, which is looser and can easily be removed from the baby's throat by the medical professionals at hand.) Yes, I was born with a kind of Gordian Knot around my neck. And although none of the doctors were named Alexander, and they certainly could not be considered Great in any sense of the word, they still did manage—barely—to untangle my death from life.

That's all I can stand for now. This is painful dredging.

Writing Chronicle: Night 1, 10:05 P.M.

Some people say I'm obsessed, but I'm not obsessed. I just know what I like, that's all. I have a very strong preference for one man in particular. I don't see how that's a bad thing. Yeah, okay, maybe I took things a little too far or whatever, but that's only because I'm dedicated to him, and loyal, and I would do anything for him. Normally, those are good things, right? People usually say those things are admirable or noble or whatever. But just because in my case the man happens to be Forest Whitaker, and he's a famous American actor, people say I'm crazy. They say I'm nutso. Well, I'm not crazy, I just have a very strong preference for Forest Whitaker and I'm extremely loyal to him because of that preference. No, we've never met. So what?

But you go 'head. You watch all of F-Dub's early movies. Within fifteen minutes of coming on-screen he's owning the joint. Acting Awesome-ified. It's just a fact. It's not a subjective opinion I hold that varies with the rest of the world. It's a goddamned fact. Go take a look. It's right there on the screen. You can check it out yourself. It's beautiful, when you think about it. Connecting with an audience like that, so deep, every single time. God. When I think about that ability…

It just drives me crazy sometimes. So crazy, I can't even write anymore. It extinguishes my energies to know I may never see F-Dub's wonderful acting ever again.

Writing Chronicle: Day 2, 3:05 A.M.

However, despite the initial handicap of being what's colloquially known as a "Nukie Baby," I survived, overcoming, so far as the medical people could tell us, any serious long-term physical effects of the condition. That was *their* opinion, anyway. I might think differently, but I have not yet attended medical school. Plus, they never even considered the mental effects *of* the physical effects. But that's medicine for you, specialized to the point of impotence.

Despite these reassurances by the medical professionals, I was then, again, in and out of hospitals as what the doctors like to euphemistically call a "sick child." The result of this period of hospitalization was more needlesticks than any child should ever be forced to go through. I recall temper tantrums, crying fits, physical fights with my mother—anything, *any*thing not to have to get more shots. But these battles I always lost, of course. Because the adults know best, and they can physically overpower a small child, even one throwing a violent temper tantrum. So again ladies and gentlemen, please (if you would) use your powers of imagination to envision being a small, worldview-limited child and having adults regularly sticking you with sharp needles. How do you think this would make you feel about the mysterious world you live in. Comfy?

Despite the needlestick ordeal, my parents still had more pain in store for me. They decided to hire some sick fucking pedophile to come along and chop off a part of my penis in what should rightly be called genital mutilation of a child, but is more commonly known in the United States of America as "circumcision." (Always nice to dress up child mutilation blood rituals in fancy-ass language, I guess.) How do you think that disgusting, excruciating event affected my epigenetics and my subconscious beliefs about what this world is and how the world treats children? Genitally mutilating a child so that when he gets older, and for the rest of his life, his sexual pleasure is irreparably diminished? What message does that send to a little boy? I ask you. What message does that send, truly? It's a world of pain and bloodshed and unspeakable horrors perpetrated by adults unto their own children. And nothing is done; nobody cares; no redress is even discussed, let alone implemented. Where is the compassion for this genital holocaust from those who claim to be compassionate peoples? Democrats, Christians, PETA people—all those who claim to speak for voiceless victims of all kinds are silent on this one while we hack away at kids with impunity.

I can't even write anymore today. That's all I can do for now. It's just too much.

Writing Chronicle: Night 2, 10:05 p.m.

I'm not crazy. Really. I just get excited sometimes. Everyone gets excited sometimes, don't they? I mean, when you think about? Doesn't everyone get excited? The world can be so dreary and humdrum all the time. Isn't excitement what people are looking for? Aren't they really dying for some excitement? So, I get excited. It's no big deal. Some people even like it that way, being around people who are excited. Excitement is exciting.

Did you know how F-Dub got his start? Oh, oh, wait. Did you know F-Dub was in a movie, *Twisted Fantasy*, with my friend Kevin Sussman? It's true. Yeah, the Kevin Sussman from Park Slope, Brooklyn. I'm not making this up. You can watch the damn thing on Netflix. K-Suss! That dude is omnipresent in the film industry. Good ol' K-Suss. Well, he's a friend of a friend, actually. A friend of a former friend. We had a kind of a falling out over the whereabouts of a certain firearm and the price of delivery for a certain green plant deemed illegal by, well, you know who. But that's not important. Just forget that part of the story.

Now F-Dub, he's the kind of dude you could be chilling with anywhere and be happy. I mean it. Like, if you were on the urine-smelly subway with him, you wouldn't even notice the urine smell too much because you'd be having such a good time. If you were sitting on some building's steps in TriBeCa, say, you wouldn't even care that you couldn't afford to live in that building even if you quadrupled your salary. You could be playing handball in the P.S. 207 schoolyard and be having the god-damned time of your life, just because he was your bro, ya know? You could be at the smelliest A&P you've ever been in, and it'd be okay cuz you'd just make fun of it. You'd make fun of everything. See, that's the kind of thing you get with F-Dub that you don't get with other dudes.

Wait. Wait a minute. Do you think K-Suss ever smoked up with F-Dub? Oh my God, I just thought of that. He probably did. I mean, they weren't in any scenes together, but so what, he was probably chilling in his trailer, and F-Dub would be all like, "Wanna blaze?" It's so natural and obvious. But that was, like, 2002. It's ancient history. Who cares? Who cares? That's not important. I mean, yeah, K-Suss got to blaze up with the Awesomeness that is F-Dub, but so what? How can you blame the guy? Such is the world of F-Dub Coolness, such is the state of affairs. It's important not to dwell on such things. It's important to stay focused. Focused. So, you probably want to know what happened with the Academy building and all that. Right. Yes.

But I can't write anymore tonight, after thinking about K-Suss and F-Dub smoking up without me. It just hurts too much. I'll have to get back to that. I'll have to get back to these dark corners of my mind at another point in time.

Writing Chronicle: Day 3, 3:05 A.M.

So, let's return to the fascinating world of epigenetics, the environment changing D.N.A. and beliefs, shall we? Especially because both of those things directly control actions. After they barbarically hacked an important portion of my penis off, and after I got well enough to be at home for good instead of living in the ever-present Pine-Sol stench of a hospital, I then was treated to a steady stream of second-hand cigarette smoke courtesy of my mother's three-pack-a-day habit. Let's face it, it's kind of a miracle I've survived. (I realize this may come off as whiny, but these are the real circumstances of my life, and if they are not fully considered, how can you, as a member of the Parole Board, completely contemplate my culpability for my crime(s)?)

Granted, less was known back then about the dangers of smoking, so some latitude must be given to my mother's disgusting addiction, but the effects of a constant gray ring around the ceiling of the house shouldn't be minimized. Is it possible that all of that smoke arrested my brain development? How about all of the cigarettes she puffed while I was in her tummy? Surely all of this must have warped my brain to some degree? And who should be held accountable for that? I ask you. Is it right to hold me accountable for neurological development problems caused by my mother's addiction to nicotine? I rather think not—and I'm the one who's lucky to be able to think at all, after all that nicotine abuse! For all of you board members who can presumably think more clearly than I can, this should be quite obvious. I pray that you deeply consider your healthful privilege in this area and have mercy upon those who have less brain health than you do.

Writing Chronicle: Night 3, 10:05 P.M.

Back in 2004, Mr. Forest Whitaker, who is an American actor from Carson, California (but born in Longview, Texas) that I happen to like a lot, as you may recall, was nominated for an Antoinette Perry Award for Excellence in Theater for his role of Bobby Majai in the play "Midnight Hallucinations and Absinthe Dreams." That's a "Tony Award," in case you were wondering. It's given out by the American Theater Wing and The Broadway

League, also known as a bunch of phony rich people who all inherited their money from people who actually took risks and made stuff happen in the real-world free market. Anyway, Mr. Whitaker lost, even though he very much deserved to win, in my opinion. And I should know because I saw that play thirty-three times, thirty-three days in a row. I was a certified expert in that particular field of knowledge.

Now, the American Theater Wing, they're housed in a building over there on 54th and 8th. And so I just went down there after the awards were announced to explain things and give them a piece of my mind, since I was so knowledgeable about the excellence of Mr. Whitaker's performance. As an expert in the field, I owed them that much.

I was, by the way, able to contain my anger over this voting malfeasance to the point where I didn't even hurt anybody inside of that office—the non-voting people, like, the receptionist, the other people walking around (I don't know what they did, what their titles were)–none of those ladies and gentlemen. Eventually, after three hours of them ignoring me and leaving me sitting in the hallway on a grey metal folding chair without so much as an offer of a cup of coffee, I just quickly and quietly walked out of there with an intense kind of burning in my chest, just the same as you would. They wouldn't even let me in to talk to anybody about this serious matter of awards malfeasance! Can you believe that? They just kept me sitting there, with my ass killing me in this metal chair they had, for like three damn hours! Well, that's no way to treat someone. It's rude, really. They've got no manners whatsoever. Isn't that rude? Isn't that the rudest thing you've ever heard about? Making a gentleman wait that long? Isn't that something? It's a slap in the face is what it is. They slapped me in the face (and the ass!) What would you do if an institution like that slapped *you* in the damned face and ass? You'd probably be mad, right? So, I got a little upset, too. I'm not going to lie. Getting slapped in the face and ass like that made me feel a burning, violent rage. An intense, boiling rage. But I was able to control it. I walked right out of that building without incident, and down into the subway without incident, and rode it all the way home, all the way back to Brooklyn, without incident. And then I plotted my revenge.

I have to go now because recalling the rage is making me upset. My shrinks here say that when I get upset I should walk around or something, and let it subside, let it calm down inside of me. In my cell, there's not much walking around that can be done, so I'm going to do push-ups until my arms collapse and I pass out. I'll return to this later. Excuse me.

Writing Chronicle: Day 4, 3:05 A.M.

But getting back to the nightmare of my childhood, constantly enveloped by a cloud of 1970s cigarette smoke, I nonetheless grew at the more-or-less normal rate for a seemingly healthy American boy. At some point during this time, my father's business started failing. (Not that I knew this at the time it was happening.) His business was designing and constructing men's apparel store window displays. The idea was, the classier the window, the more customers the store would attract. Retail clothing stores, or at least the kind of mom-and-pop stores my dad worked with, however, began flocking out of New York City or closing shop and there started to be less of a need for the kinds of services he provided to those businesses. I'm no Paul Krugman, but I think it had to do with taxes or something. Anyways, when that happened, my father decided to fill his new-found free time by drinking large quantities of alcohol and watching television. My mother disagreed with this decision, and that led to many fights between them on a near-daily basis. These fights were generally conducted with the volume knob dialed to "The Neighbors Are Seriously Concerned." For me, they simply meant cowering in my room, praying for the madness to end.

Surely, living amid intense domestic violence and random, thumping noises at all hours of the day and night couldn't possibly have affected my mental health. Could it? Nah. I'm sure all of the board members had lovely, peaceful childhoods, but it wasn't like that for all of us. I ask you simply to consider a reality outside of your experience. Is that so difficult to comprehend?

Writing Chronicle: Night 4, 10:05 P.M.

So, after the awards people wouldn't take a meeting with me at their office, I figured out that I had to get their attention in order to right this egregious wrong about F-Dub's Tony loss. I did some scoping out of the place. Their building, it's got some decent layers of defense, for sure. After 9/11, everyone got busy hardening themselves and whatnot. So, there are some bullocks by the curb, a large planter fifteen feet in front of the front entrance, a few trees in the sidewalk, the curb (obviously), and that's it for the street-facing perimeter defenses. That's all cool anyway because I wasn't planning a car bomb or anything like that. Car bombs are hard to manage for one person and there's really way too much collateral damage, potentially. You have to think about shattered glass radii, and structural collapse which can mean bricks flying everywhere, and you just have too many damn people who can be injured or killed who aren't your targets. I wasn't interested in any of that—I'm reasonable, after all. I just wanted to make sure the voters understood just how vital their votes were. They had profound effects on society, and I knew that if we forgot that lesson, then everything could be lost.

Other than that, the building has some decent secondary defense layers, such as rent-a-cops all along the entrance, and a sign-in security desk. They also have cameras located at points along the entrance and the interior sign-in area. I scoped all of this out on a couple of reconnaissance missions I did, no big deal really. Anyone who's paying attention to their environment could do the same thing. It's not James Bond stuff.

The building envelope is typical for a commercial building of its size being a three-story 30,000 square-foot corner building with underground parking facilities. Exterior walls are red brick with joisted masonry and the roof appeared to be level with about a one-foot parapet surrounding it. Incoming water supply is hard to identify and therefore secure. Other utilities such as natural gas, telephone lines, computer lines, and electricity supplied by ConEd all pose the problem of unintended consequences with regard to non-target individuals, businesses, and nearby municipal operations, so I didn't analyze those too much.

After thinking about it some, it seemed to me that there was only one realistic opportunity that didn't run the risk of collateral damage: the air intake system, which was located on the 8th Avenue side of the building and was completely unguarded. For things like this, the simpler the better, I thought. I couldn't assemble an *Oceans Eleven* team or anything, so complexity was not my friend.

From my Internet research, I determined that people seem to make a distinction between chemical and biological. "Nuclear Biological Chemical" gear, for example, is how the military thinks of it. I make no such distinction because a chemical agent—say, chlorine—will affect your body on a biological level, and all the way down to the nucleus of your cells. So, it's really all the same thing, in a way. The only factor that's really important is the amount of harm you can do with any given substance. How much damage can you cause? *That's* the important thing, really. Also, how much (what quantity) of a certain substance is required to affect the level of damage you're looking to inflict? This is almost always expressed as X parts per million. So, what I learned online is that the trick really is all about getting that X expressed correct. If you do, you can be successful. If you *don't*, then all you've done is take on a ton of risk for no good reason, and possibly caused some mild annoyances. It's not worth it. So, the task, then, is to figure out how to determine X.

Chlorine, in certain quantities and concentrations, is categorized by the Centers for Disease Control as a Category B biological agent. This means it has the potential for large-scale dissemination with resultant illness, but generally causes less illness and death than Category A biological agents. When places like the United States of America Department of Homeland Security ranks chlorine on the basis of specific criteria, each criterion being ranked on a 1-10 scale, chlorine ends up with a final score of 40. That's not an extreme score, but it is on the higher side of other agents like phosgene, hydrogen cyanide, lewisite, sarin, and so on.

The other thing about chlorine is that it's readily available for purchase at any number of retailers wherever you may happen to be. So, I think you can see where this is headed, plot-wise. It's not exactly a mystery here.

Writing Chronicle: Mid-Day, Day X

When I woke up that morning it wasn't the first time I'd woken up that day. I'd been getting up all night. My bed sheets were drenched with sweat and my pillow smelled like a wet dog. I kept wondering, as I laid there a few minutes before my alarm would go off, about what would become of the five framed Forest Whitaker posters in my bedroom. My mom would probably figure out that she needed to account for my stuff, but since we rarely spoke anymore, I just didn't know for sure.

I finally got up for good at 4:05 A.M. I felt nervous, yet focused. It was still dark out. I walked through my bedroom's pink door jamb and stumbled my way into the kitchen, which had three of the brown-, tan-, and orange-swirl linoleum tiles misaligned, with the black mastic exposed. I'd never gotten around to fixing them, and I never would.

I looked at the three glue traps I had spread around the kitchen. Two of them contained barely-wriggling, little grey field mice in them. I grabbed a long metal rod I kept around for this exact purpose. I looked away as I pushed the rod down into the first and then the second field mouse. I did this until I felt no more movement in their struggling, desperate-for-life bodies. I snapped on yellow rubber gloves and dropped their bodies and traps into black plastic bags, tying the bag-handles together. I dumped them into the garbage.

I made a full pot of coffee, and boiled water for my spaghetti. In a small pot, I poured some canned Hormel chili and began to heat it up. A "chighetti" breakfast bolstered by black coffee always made me feel invincible; it was also excellent sustenance for days when the next meal's timing was unknowable.

After I showered and dressed, I walked downstairs, each wooden step in the narrow stairwell hallway creaky and echoey, and opened the front door. Flatbush Avenue was still bathed in darkness and streetlamp-light, providing a superficial kind of shadowy atmosphere in the quiet of the desolate morning. Across the street, a darkened funeral home loomed above the deserted, black-top avenue. Behind it lay a still-as-stone cemetery next to a rotting, dilapidated church.

The air smelled of asphalt, grime, and urine. A narrow stream of dripped-down air-conditioning water snaked in front of my feet on the gum- and grit-dappled sidewalk. I felt one last twinge of anxiety before taking in a long breath of dirty Brooklyn air. I locked the graffiti-stained door behind me, turned, and walked past the A/C water toward the descending stairs of the Shroud Street subway station.

8.
Valhalla House

"No, homie. But it's not my call."

The words felt heavy to Enzo, as if they had separated themselves from ordinary language, figured out how to accumulate gravitas, and then used this extra heft to demolish him. He sat down on the orange couch in the common area of the suite. (The next day, the school would be refreshing the suite by switching out the couch for a newer, less embarrassing one.) Enzo shook his shaggy-haired head in disbelief. Steve Thorson of the Short Hills Thorsons, captain of the college's golf club, had just let loose the barrage of heavy-artillery verbiage. He was also playing *Tiger Woods PGA Tour* on his X-Box. "Look," Thorson said, "we all heard that message from your buddy, whatshisname. Rolf or whatever. Sounds like you guys are getting a nice little house of your own. So, don't complain. Out-compete."

"You do understand endorsements come back, right?" Enzo said. "They. Come. Back. When I'm ready to go, they'll all come back. You hear me?"

"All," Steve said, mockingly blowing air our of his sunburnt nose. "I'm killing it right now. Just gotta....nail...this...putt." His fingers click-clacked the game controller, leaving a staccato echo lingering in the air.

"Nike's coming back at least," Enzo said, defensively, exhaustedly.

"I'm trying to play here, dude," Thorson said, eyes fixed on the Samsung 32-inch LED Hi-Def TV. He ran a hand through the right side of his straight blonde hair. "Nike's with everyone.

Nike's not a market differentiator anymore, to tell you the truth. Used to be, but not anymore." Steve swiveled his black Aeron office chair with a red hockey jersey laid over the back of it toward Enzo, and winked at him. The jersey had white numbers and letters. The numbers and letters said, "THORSON. 13."

Enzo shook his head slowly, thinking about what being exiled from the group of the school's best athletes would mean, and what it would feel like. Wincing as if in physical pain, he lifted a bottle of Pabst Blue Ribbon from the beat-up coffee table in front of him and drank down about a quarter of the bottle. He put it back on the table. "Lemme ask you something, Steve."

"Okay, shoot," Steve said. "Wait, lemme pause this. Okay. Go."

"Are you an idiot?" Enzo said. He heard, low and distant from one of the interior rooms off the suite, the song "Splendid Isolation" by Warren Zevon, but not the original version, the cover off the posthumous tribute album, *Enjoy Every Sandwich*.

"Come on, man," Thorson said. "Don't be like that. You know how it is."

"Like what?"

"Like *that*," Thorson said. "You know what I mean. A fake victim. Bootstraps, ingenuity, all that. Be entrepreneurial, Enzo! Every challenge is an opportunity. C'mon, man, you know all this stuff."

"What are you doing listening to *my* phone messages anyway?" Enzo said. "Did you get Low-Key to hack my phone or something?"

Thorson unpaused the video game and started playing again. "You guys can probably get a little love nest right down the street or something," Thorson said. "No big deal. We can have dueling parties or something."

"Mmhmm," said Enzo, with sarcasm dripping from his voice. "I know what's really going on."

"What's really going on, Enzo?"

"You guys think I'm washed up, just because I picked up a few el-bees or whatever," Enzo said. "You're gonna go get some nice house in town and call it Elite Jock House or some stupid crap like that, and you don't want...whatever, man. You guys think you're slick, but you're not so slick, you know that?"

"Enzo, man, come on," said Steve. "You know it's not like that. And it's not my call, anyway. You should be bitching to Odinberger, not me! He's the C.E.O. of this stuff!"

Enzo snatched his beer from the coffee table and gurgled the rest of the bottle down his angry throat. He got up, walked over to the mini-fridge in the corner of the common area, grabbed and opened a new one. He peeled the label off of it and shoved it in his back jeans pocket. He was saving all of the labels of all of the beer bottles he drank during his recovery from Tommy John surgery. The labels were a weird kind of talisman representing all the people who loved him fifty pounds and a 95 mile-an-hour fastball ago, the people who were abandoning him now.

"You might wanna throttle it back there, chief," Thorson said. "It's only eleven in the morning or whatever it is."

Enzo stood there watching Steve Thorson play his little game. "You guys are bunch of fucking dicks, you're aware of that, right?" he said.

Steve clicked and clacked on his controller, watching the brightness of the television screen flicker and dance. "Don't worry," he said after blowing a two-foot putt. "You can come over *any* time you want, big boy."

Enzo walked over to Steve, turned, and farted in his face.

With moonlight reflecting off his Ball mason jar full of beer-bottle labels, Enzo found it hard to sleep that night. His head, after eight bottles of Pabst Blue Ribbon, felt unsteady, like the mental version of a drunk's swaying walk. He felt fine for a while, then his mind would slip for a second, and then correct itself again. Despite this, his thoughts were not wobbly. Crystal-clear visions of setting fire to houses sparked in his mind. He could inhale the smell of the smoke, feel the deliciously acrid taste of it on his tongue. He hugged the waves of warmth spraying from the flickering flames. His pride expanded with the blooming power of controlling nature. He felt as if he were wallowing in the destructive love the fire created.

Just as he was savoring that feeling of power, he heard the heaviness of footsteps approaching, footsteps that could only belong to someone the size and heft of his roommate and catcher, Lakewood "Semzy" Semend. The loud footsteps clopped into the room from the common area. They paused near Semzy's closet.

Although Enzo's mind was in a hypnagogic state of dreams and visions, sleep and wakefulness, he didn't stir from his twin bed. He stayed still as stone, listening. His fire-dreams faded.

Semzy, Enzo heard, snapped off his gold watch and placed it down on his desk. He snipped off his silver earrings and placed them down. He rummaged his toiletries kit from his closet and walked toward the door. "Valhalla House," he whispered to himself. "God-damn." He walked out.

The idea of a "Valhalla House" made Enzo feel scared, deep-down scared in ways he usually used large quantities of beer to hide. He could feel the impact of losing everything—way more important stuff than the free gear sports equipment companies provided. For instance: The way almost every girl on campus looked at him (head down, eyes up) and NOT at the guy next to him; the leniency of the grades he received; the deference paid to him by other guys on campus. If he wasn't in Valhalla House, he knew it was all over. He would be just another chump with nowhere to call home. He knew, too, that his emotions were being melodramatic, silly, but they seemed to subsume him anyway.

He turned toward his side, and his head hit the pillow feeling heavy, a sort of repressed depression refusing to be repressed anymore. It felt like all of his dreams were dying. He knew, too, that that was pathetic, but even knowing it couldn't prevent the sadness.

The next day Enzo made a few phone calls, then drove down to his family's house in Brooklyn, on Violinn Street, where he grew up. Enzo sat down at the south end of the dining room table with an unopened bottle of Pabst Blue Ribbon in front of him. His six-year-old sister, Maya, came rushing—on her blinking sneaker-toes—into the room. "Enzo got fat at college!

Mom! Enzo got fat at college!" She hurried out—on her sneaker-heels—to find their mother, or anyone else to whom to spill this big secret. It had only been four months since the surgery, but Enzo had taken the opportunity to expand the concept of the "Freshman Fifteen."

The mid-morning sunlight streamed in from the north window through a fading-white semi-sheer curtain, bringing with it memories of family breakfasts full of pancakes, and milky cereal, and bacon and eggs. The house was quiet, but Enzo could somehow hear the echoes of distant noises from his childhood—the way the basement metal sump basin cover sounded when you stepped on it, the creek and splunk of the basement stairs, the sing-song chime of the doorbell. All of these things felt real to Enzo, felt in the present moment, but they were not. They were gone, except for their residue on his memory.

He looked over at the west wall, the southern half of which was decorated with a wooden crosshatch latticework pattern, although it was barely intact now. It used to be quite decorative, he remembered, but now it suffered from splintered jagged edges, burn marks, and fading black, red, and blue marks that would be difficult to trace back to their sources. The kitchen adjoined the dining room to the west through the moulding-free archway. A tan rotary phone, back in time, on the wall just inside the kitchen, appeared in Enzo's mind. He recalled its thousand-foot-long, twirly cord often snaking past his smoking mother in a lavender house coat and white slippers; his brother and three friends in St. Michael's baseball uniforms; his father drinking Schlitz at the card table with his buddies. (Enzo remembered hating his dad for those card games because he wanted—in fact, tantrum-begged—his dad to drive him to the batting cages.) Other times, Dad would get home from work, crack open a Schlitz, get on the phone, and not stop talking until he passed out drunk, forgetting all about Enzo's pleas to hit the cages. Anytime Enzo "aksed" him about it, he'd say he needed to "check in" with as many people as possible because it was good for business. "Goo' fah bizniz, Enzie!" he'd say.

The phone itself was tan, Enzo remembered, fading toward cream. Enzo looked up at the spot on the wall where the phone should have been, or rather used to be. Now, there was simply a grey metal rectangle about five inches long and four inches wide, with a telephone-jack hole stabbed in the middle of it. The metal rectangle's left top corner was tattered down, with a few millimeters of lighter, duller grey creeping through. On the right bottom corner bled a light red stain, fading daily into a kind of off-red.

His brother, Gabriel, was talking to him now, it seemed. "What?" Enzo said, snapping it off, as if to break himself out of his own remembrance fog.

"How's the rehab going, jeez," Gabriel said. "You're like lost over there." Gabriel drank from a large brown bottle of Arrogant Bastard Ale.

"Huh?" Enzo said. "Oh, uh, yeah. It's fine. That's fine, Gabe."

"Ralphie's here," Gabriel said. "You might wanna think about talking to Dad tonight. He said he wants to talk to you." He picked up his 32-ounce bottle of Arrogant Bastard Ale and walked downstairs, to his recently renovated basement apartment.

Raphael Mendez walked in and sat down at the table.

"You want a beer or something?" Enzo said. "We got beer."

"Sure," said Raphael.

Enzo got him one and put it in front of him on the table.

Raphael twisted it open. Enzo watched the little white cloud emerge from the bottle top, as Raphael spun the cap on the table like a dreidel.

"So," Raphael said. "I heard you're not pitching anymore."

"Kinda hard to pitch after they slice open your elbow."

"Right. So, why not come back down, transfer to CCNY with me and Bob Haniel? We could get a house in Queens and live like kings."

"Why Queens?"

"I got some fam out there," said Raphael. "They'd give us some space."

"So, it'd be, like, me, you, Haniel, and some random members of your family?" Enzo said. "That sounds somewhat less than appealing."

"No, it'd be great!" Raphael said. "We wouldn't have to pay too much rent, and we'd be on campus most of the time, anyway."

"Mmhmm," Enzo said. "You came up with this little plan all by yourself, did you?" Enzo had quit the USSBL team he and Raphael had started so that he could concentrate on his college career. As teenagers, they had led the team to a 14-1 record in its second season and a playoff run, which ended in a disappointing walk-off walk.

"Yeah, and listen, we could totally dominate the Queens Division if you came back. You can't pitch, but you can still hit, right? Me and Haniel can pitch, and we'll dominate the hell out of it."

"Of course I can still hit," Enzo said. "But wait a minute, wait a minute. Why doesn't anyone get this? Tommy John surgery heals, usually in, like, eighteen months. And most guys come back just as good as before, if not better. Why am I gonna transfer to CCNY and live with a bunch of random people in some bunkhouse in Queens when I'll be fine in about a year anyway?" Enzo heard the creek and thumps of his sister Maya running around upstairs, carefree and wide-eyed with wonder about everything. Enzo missed those cigarette-smoke-shrouded days—the days when he didn't have anything valuable, so no one wanted anything from him.

"No!" Raphael protested. "You're forgetting about how cool it'll be to live with us, and also, too, to dominate the league. What good is playing for New Paltz, when you could dominate down here? Dominate, don't just participate, that's what I'm talkin' about."

Enzo rolled his eyes. "Dominate the Queens Division? Stickball?"

"Yah!" said Raphael.

"Ralphie," Enzo said, "You're a smart guy. You didn't ask me to come down here to talk about stickball and CCNY. You sure there's not a Dodgeball League somewhere you wanna promote?"

"No, I really think you're missing out on having fun playing..."

"Oh, that's bullshit," Enzo said. "Let's be honest. You just want me to start seeing Cristiana again, so you can have a way in with her sister Rosa."

"Nah, dude," Raphael said. He looked down at the table and then, as if catching himself, looked quickly back up at his beer bottle. He drank down a big swig of beer.

"You can't admit you're too chicken to just go right up to Rosa and ask her out. You always gotta have a backdoor way, cuz you think she's outta your league. That's the way it is with you. Why don't you try, like, being a man for once? Be aggressive. Maybe she'll take pity on your ass or something."

"That's ridiculous," Raphael said. "Hey. Hey." His voice cracked, as if changing the subject so quickly caused a physical reaction in his vocal cord. "You hear about Robbie Borr?"

"No, what?"

"He blew out his arm again. Needs another surgery."

"Again? Damn."

"Yeah," Raphael said. "He had gotten back up to like 88, 89 miles an hour. But now? He's pretty much toast, I think."

"So what's he gonna do?"

"Hell if I know. Business major, I guess."

"Damn."

"That could be you, Enzo," Raphael said. "Just sayin'. Two surgeries, and that's pretty much it. That's all you get. Might as well come home, have as much fun as you can while your arm holds up, dude."

That night, Enzo cancelled the plans he had to meet up with Raphael and Bob Haniel for a drink or five. Instead, he drove back up to New Paltz. He pulled into the parking lot with his fuel needle dangerously close to E.

He plopped down on the ratty, orange, common-area couch, which still hadn't been switched out. "Semzy, are you gonna move into Valhalla House?" Enzo said as he pulled a can of Pabst Blue Ribbon from the mini-fridge in the Bevier suite.

"They want me to," Semzy said, standing in the doorway of their room, holding on to the pull-up bar in a red, ribbed tank top.

"Yeah," Enzo said.

"But I don't think so."

"Why not?" Enzo said.

"My dad, he's a stockbroker, right?" said Semzy.

"Bulls and bears," Enzo said.

"Right," Semzy said. "Aaaand he always told me—when a market starts to move one way or another, you need to know why it's moving. Otherwise, you try to ride a wave, but you just get trampled on, sort of." He pulled himself up on the bar, and knocked out fifteen quick pull-ups.

"Know what my dad told me?" Enzo said.

"What?"

"Gimme your paper-route money, Enzie," Enzo said, imitating his father's deep, accented voice. "Daddy's cash-poor and needs a label for his collection. That's what he called a beer, a label for his collection."

"Why?" Semzy said.

"Who the hell knows."

Semzy sighed. "Moving on from your childhood drama, Enzo, the point is this. I've come to have this crazy ability to take a long position whereas most people, especially dickhead young jocks, they're all about moving around in the shorts." He dropped off the pull-up bar, and suddenly stabbed his hand into his front jeans-shorts pocket. He yanked out his cell phone, and lasered an angry look at it. "Damn crazy bitch won't let a nigga be." He spiked his cell phone into the exposed concrete floor, a smile blossoming on his face.

"Now how are you gonna, like, communicate?" Enzo said.

"Let's go get a label," Semzy said.

For the uninitiated, and because we like to be helpful, here now are some useful rules of thumb about postmodern literary stories. The stories can include the following techniques, which should be kept in mind at all times if the reader wishes to have a mental orgasm at the conclusion of the story: Irony or playfulness; lack of traditional storytelling techniques such as an engaging plot; fragmentation; chaos; metafiction; lack of rising tension and conflict; temporal distortion; hyper-reality; magic realism; paranoia; lack of characters overcoming obstacles; maximalism; and, minimalism. Our two writers (heroes, really) in the following story didn't know about these techniques at the time, however. They wouldn't even recognize the fact that this very introduction represents an element of postmodern writing in and of itself. It's okay, though, because that's why we have an objective omniscient narrator, who helps us carry that weight. It's all very profound and thought-provoking and orgasmic. The handsome and charming young man who authored this one certainly must be some kind of sexy super-genius.

9.

Eroticoffica

"Jessa, I think you're really…I dunno," said Becky. "You're kind of pushing it a little hard, know what I mean?"

Jessa Tarsdale and Becky O'Tackley were walking down toward Lamar from "The Castle" on Ann Arky Street. The Castle was a big house that looked, from certain angles, like a castle. But it wasn't a castle. It was just a regular house at the top of an inclined Austin, Texas street. Kind of.

"We….you can't tell me you don't feel it," Jessa said. It was a typical summer morning in Austin, ninety-three degrees with a searing humidity under an unrelentingly bright sun.

"Oh, c'mon," Becky said. "How can you be feeling like it's not a great situation?"

"Really?" Jessa said. "Don't you think it's a little unusual?" Jessa was wearing her black-based workout outfit, a tank top over a sports bra, jogging shorts, and New Balance running sneakers.

"But Asha…." said Becky. "She totally takes care of us. And I mean, look what she's done for our writing. You think we'd be where we are without her?" Becky was in a similar outfit as her B.F.F., except it was based more in yellows and oranges.

Jessa and Becky, it should be stated right here near the outset, were "Kindle Millionaires." This was a millennial kind of *nouveau riche* made possible by the revolution of Amazon.com-led self-publishing and the market acceptance of new e-reading devices. The girls, within six months of graduating from the University of Texas at Austin (English majors), had found success through different sub-genres of erotica in e-readerland. Erotica at this time represented tens of millions of total book sales per year in the United States of America alone. The Castle was a combination boarding house and work space where twenty young female erotica authors lived, each cranking out many titles of hot-selling erotica each year. The writers received their orders via an e-mail they had to retrieve by 8 A.M. each morning, and then it was straight keyboard click-clacking all day long, with a thirty minute break for lunch. Non-compliance with the rules was enforced by paycheck deductions.

"Sure," said Jessa. "Why not? It's not that hard to run a digital publishing house, y'know."

"Oh please," said Becky. "What about the marketing, blog tours, all that stuff? Think you could do all that yourself?"

Jessa said, "You....you're getting confused. I think you're confusing discipline with with I dunno.... Like forced labor! Slavery! That's it! We're Asha's little word slaves! That's exactly what we are!"

"You're being dramatic, Jessa," Becky said. "You, me, any of us! We can leave any time we want! It's probably coming from your stories, I bet. Like, what are you working on right now?"

"The sixties," said Jessa.

"The nineteen sixties?" said Becky.

"I've never done one in that era, though."

"Should be fun," Becky said. "Peace, love, and erotica!"

"Yeah, but check it out, though," said Jessa. "It's about this couple who are like totally bored of the whole peace, drugs, and hippy sex thing..."

"Who'd get bored with that?" said Becky. "We need *more* drugs, like caffeine..."

"So, they start having sex *only* through a board," said Jessa.

"A board," said Becky, skeptically.

"Yeah, this pretty thin board, like, with a hole in it," said Jessa. "It's pretty hawt."

"Um, okay?"

"Trust me, I'll make it work," said Jessa. "When you've written as much historical erotica as I have, you start looking for other, like, some alternative stuff. I'm so tired of writing these historical people having kinky sex. I mean, it was cool the first ten books, but I mean, you gotta change it up sometimes, you know? Teddy Roosevelt, bend over *again*....Jeez, it gets boring!"

"Wait," said Becky. "Where are you taking me? You said we were going to the best coffee place, but you didn't say where it was or anything like that."

"Becky, ohmygod you have *got* to try this coffee place on Lamar. It is sooooo Awesome-Austin!"

Becky, a little spooked despite their new clique-phrase, said, "Awesome-Austin? Does it serve breakfast tacos?"

"Nooo, you get your food, like, next door, at Mickey D's!"

"Mickey D's?" said Becky.

"Yeah, yeah. It's totally like a thing. Trust me."

"Okay, I guess. Lead on McMuff!"

"The Place," as it was known, was the plainest-looking coffee shop in Austin, and maybe the world. It consisted of a whiteish, greyish building underneath a huge yellow canopy next to an ordinary McDonald's on South Lamar Boulevard. There was a small, hand-written sign, taped up to the wall near the ordering window to keep people from wandering around in confusion more than anything else, that said, "Coffee," with an arrow pointing to the window. There were no kiosks full of condiments; no trash bins; no food displays. All of the tables and chairs were outside, under the canopy. Gypsy jazz music floated through the air, but if you tried to find where the sounds were actually coming from, you'd drive yourself into *The Conversation*-like insanity. On those rare rainy or frost-cold days in Austin, The Place would mysteriously close—no sign would be posted, but the ordering window would be locked. The Place, of course, had no website, no Twitter account, no Instagram. In short, it seemed—on certain heat-advisory days—like The Place was a coffee oasis in the middle of Desert Lamar and that through its brown elixirs one could attain for a small price a little cup of salvation.

The Place had one employee, the proprietor, Ms. Resurreccion. On the day that Becky and Jessa entered the oasis under the yellow canopy and walked up to the window, Ms. Resurreccion wore white lipstick, white eye shadow, and a white carnation in her hair. She took their "orders" (more on this later) and the girls sat down at one of the rickety, round, metal tables under the yellow canopy. They placed their paper-wrapped Egg McMuffins on the table.

Jessa stood up and approached a man in a yellow T-shirt who was sitting alone, drinking coffee, and reading a book entitled, *Rules of the Game*. "Excuse me, sir," she said.

The man looked up, a little startled. But then he smiled as he realized a cute young lady had approached him, perhaps for the first time in his life. His eyes belted out that this surprising churn of events promised to turn *everything* around, as if he had just started a positive-thinking regimen, and this chance encounter proved the fruit of all his mental labor would be manna-like. "Yes?" he said with a hopeful lilt in his voice, full of the sort of optimism that virtually screamed from the rooftops about how Jessa asking him out would make his life feel like complete and total love.

Jessa said, "Would you buy an erotica novel that takes place in the sixties, and that's about a couple who has hardcore sex through a hole in a board?"

The man in the yellow T-shirt's eyes lit up, as if he had just hit the existential lottery. "Sure!" he said, almost falling out of his chair with excitement. The excitement radiated off of him in vibrant waves, like heat off the road in Phoenix, Arizona.

"Thanks," Jessa said. She turned around and walked away from the man.

The man looked utterly stunned, as if he knew his only chance for happiness had barely slipped through his desperate fingers. Later in the day he would end his life by way of brain-bullet, but no one who knew him could quite figure out why. Everything had seemed to be going so well for him, they would all say in one form or another, heads shaking dutifully. He finally felt comfortable enough to buy and wear that yellow T-shirt that he'd wanted forever, but had felt embarrassed about, for some reason. In any event, the man and his yellow, blood-splattered T-shirt were dead.

Jessa walked back to her table with Becky. "See," she said, jerking a thumb in the direction of the man. "He'd buy it."

"That's not exactly, like, good marketing research."

"Why not? I liked it. I think it's pretty good." Jessa felt a kind of craftsperson's pride, the kind that fills you up with satisfaction after looking at the finished product of the work, the toil, the hours' worth of labor. It was almost tangible, even though it was not. And that feeling of "almost," that near-reality, made Jessa tingle with the pleasure of being teased.

"Jessa, it's really amazing you can write erotica so well," Becky said. "You really have no idea how men's minds work, do you?"

Jessa said, "I do so! I know a lot of things you think I don't know about!"

"Like what?"

"Men are so easy to understand," Jessa said. "What, like they're complex or something? I mean, like, watch what they do when we're jogging in the morning. And we're just wearing shorts and sports bras! Their eyeballs, most of 'em, they pop out of their heads, almost. Like a cartoon or something. That's all you need to know about men. Eyeballs."

"Eye," Becky said. "Balls."

"Yeah! Eye. Balls!" Jessa contributed to the joint-joke. They both broke out laughing in a kind of derogatory, superior laugh that made each of them feel good and warm and safe. It was the kind of addictive feeling their decade-long friendship was based on.

Hearing the laughter of the girls was really the turning point for the man in the yellow T-shirt, however. He knew, just knew, that they were laughing at him like no man had ever been laughed at, and he just couldn't take it anymore. So, he got up and left The Place and went home and got his roommate's yellow handgun and fired a bullet through his brain. His body thudded on the floor, and that was it for him. Except for all the fake gnashing of teeth and so on by his friends and relatives, but that was pretty much it. The girls' laughter, of course, had nothing whatsoever to do with him, but the man didn't get a chance to figure that out before he decided he couldn't take the cruel, capricious joke that he perceived life to be.

For Jessa and Becky, their feeling of shared laughter was like no other feeling, or drug even, on earth. It couldn't be replaced by anything or anyone in the whole wide world, and that's what made it so special. It was better than lust, better than love, even. It was the kind of thing that made life mysterious and cool, even for young, attractive, rich erotica authors who could manipulate so much so easily. They were masters of the universe, but yet something was still wrong. Very wrong.

And *that* was why Jessa knew what she had to do was going to be the most painful thing she would ever have to feel in her entire life. Jessa had been manipulating men through their dicks for so long now that she was entirely bored with the entire male species. If she could only meet one man—just one!—who would stand up to her, to tell her *no*... ahh, now that man would be sexy as hell, sexier than any character she could create in her stories. She might just have to fall in love with him on the spot, or... Or what? She didn't know. Pass out, maybe. That might be too much drama but she knew, deep down, that she needed that kind of man. She also doubted he actually existed in America, and if he did, he certainly did not live in Austin, Texas, home of the poser-boys, hipster doofuses, and fake rock stars. She knew she needed to move on, which first meant getting herself and Becky out of the cult known as The Castle.

Jessa and Becky started kissing. Wait, no, that didn't happen. Not at all. Sorry. My bad. It *had* happened in one of the other erotica girls' stories who were fellow Castle-cult members, but that's a story for another day. It's kind of confusing, but still. It might be well worth mentioning here, though, that *that* novel sold over 100,000 copies. These kinds of things can be confusing and lucrative at the same time, especially in this postmodern era.

Becky, on the other hand, seemed to suffer from no such romantic ill effects of her success. Her dating life was rich and varied. She wrote science fiction erotica, or what some critics dismissed as simply, "Sex in Space." She didn't mind not being taken seriously—it was all pure fun and excitement and Becky loved to have fun more than anything. She always felt a nagging sense of dissatisfaction with whatever she was doing, but so long as she stayed spontaneous and unpredictable, everything worked out all right because that way, she didn't have to examine her life too deeply or worry too much about the signals her body was trying to send to her brain. She preferred day-dreaming anyway, and then putting versions of those day-dreams into her stories.

Sorry, we got a little off-track there. When Jessa and Becky, or anyone really, ordered their coffee at the window of The Place, they followed the strict rules The Place mandated. There were no signs indicating what these rules were, so the rules had to be passed along socially, with violators quickly removed from The Place by fellow patrons who understood the benefits and powers of following the rules. Violators represented a threat to their own enlightenment, and so were dealt with promptly and unambiguously. As I'm sure you can easily understand. The rules were similar to those seen on "The Soup Nazi" episode of the American television show, "Seinfeld." You walked up to the window, told Ms. Resurreccion your name and occupation, paid your two dollars cash, and then you sat down. Jessa and Becky had done so, and now were waiting on the coffee like you wait for your dinner at a restaurant.

Eventually, Ms. Resurreccion came out of a secret door holding two large coffee mugs, one snowy white and one dark brown, with white steam billowing out of them and swirling through the air, as did her flowy white dress. She placed the brown mug down in front of Becky, the white in front of Jessa. Looking at Jessa she said, "*Por tu*, powerful *cafe* bean. Pearl Mountain Indian Peaberry, shade-grown, wet-washed, roasted City Plus fullness. *Robusto* cup-flavor *y* good potency from extraction. Powerful, flavorful, not yet elegant, but close."

Looking at Becky, she said, "*Por tu*, something else. Original beans from small farm in Yemen countryside. Earthy, dirty, rooted vines for beans. Roasted to dark look and feel, Full City Plus cup flavor. This is good cup, but nasty. Enjoy."

And with that, she whisked away, back through the secret door, back to whatever she did behind it. No one really knew what that was, and no one ever cared to ask. The rituals of The Place were too sacred and effective to question their origins or mechanisms of action.

"What now?" said Becky, in a cold, hateful tone of voice. "I got Nasty." She frowned, looking cautiously at her steaming brown mug of Nasty.

"Now we drink! This is the best part," said Jessa, smiling the smile of a woman convinced of her own salvation.

"Yeah, you got Powerful," said Becky with bitterness shot through her voice. "I got Nasty from Yemen. Maybe I should drink from yours."

"No!" said Jessa. "If you do that, we'll get our asses thrown out of here by the others." There was no one else in The Place at the moment. Sensing Becky thinking this, Jessa said, "Trust me, they're like ninjas. If we screw things up, they'll, like, come outta nowhere and fling us into the street. It won't be pretty and we won't be allowed back in here, either. Everyone knows this. It's like an urban legend, except it's true."

"Okay," said Becky. "But don't you think this is all just a little strange? The McMuffins, the two dollars, the mystery coffee?"

"I love it!" said Jessa. "It's soooo Awesome-Austin."

At that precise moment, a tall, handsome, college-aged dude walked in, under the yellow tarp. He was square-jawed and athletically built. He smiled at Jessa and Becky, then walked toward them. When he got to their table, he bent down and whispered, "This place is so strange." He smiled again, then walked to the window to place his "order."

"Oh. My. Gah," said Becky.

"Pu-lease," said Jessa.

Ms. Resurreccion emerged again from the secret door. Her black hair, Jessa noticed this time, featured grungy strands of white and grey coming out from a little grey tarboosh. She walked with a slight limp and was hunched over just a little as she made her way toward Jessa and Becky. She stopped in front of Jessa and dropped something into her coffee.

"Wait, what?" Jessa said.

Becky had shifted her curiosity onto the athletic dude waiting at the window. Her eyes said she was day-dreaming. She didn't pay too much attention to Ms. Resurreccion this time. Her hands were in her lap.

Ms. Resurreccion said, "This is *not* marshmallow. No! No marshmallow! No American bullshit! It is from marsh mallow plant, but is different. *Comprende? Si?* Comes from plant near Nile *Rio*, *en* Egypt. Not processed, like stupid American marshmallows. This is mixed, *tambien*, *con* pure cane *azucar y* egg whites. Marsh mallow gives healing."

"Hilling?" said Jessica.

"Heal-ing," the old woman said. "Cures *tu* pain. Heed the healings." Ms. Resurreccion walked, slow and halting, back through the secret door.

Jessa stared down into the mug, as the white marsh mallow cube disintegrated slowly and evenly into the brown coffee. She smelled the wonderful coffee flavor and anticipated the promised healing. Feeling satisfied, images of the future flew through her mind as clear as if projected by a high-definition television program. She lifted the white mug and took a sip of the hot luscious brew. She smiled, feeling the effects more or less immediately.

10.

Conflation

My mind, I think, does this thing where it tries (with something like a fifty percent success rate) to block out painful memories, especially ones that involve mistakes that may have led to the deaths of my two best friends. So even, like now, when I need to access them, it can be somewhat rough-going. I heard somewhere that if you really want to solve a problem, you have to dig down to its root causes. That seems right to me, but it also seems to assume that objective facts *can* be determined. I'm not so sure. The thought of Ed and Josh being gone makes half of me desperately need to forget everything, and the other half desperately need to remember.

"You need to do this with us, Kronos." Ed Horndecker's voice, low, hard to hear.

My mind remembers my voice saying, "Why?" with a kind of nervous twitching in my body's gut, signaling...something. What it could be is impossible to discern. My unreliable emotions play a part in all of this, too—in this deception of self-protection—and my mind has never been particularly good at controlling those sons of bitches.

Horndecker again, it seems: "Salinger, Mailer, Hemingway, O'Brien... serving'll be good for your writing *and* your reading. The best writers were also freedom fighters."

Bullshit bullshit bullshit!

My mind tries to fight back against such falsehoods, but can't ever seem to bring the memories back into existence, let alone combat them. My mind feels constricted, tight, locked-down. It feels impotent.

Horndecker, apparently, said, "Plus, chicks dig paratroopers. How many paratroopers are they gonna meet who're also writers?"

Bullshit bullshit bullshit!

Why did my mind always let these delusions of grandeur pieces of bullshit influence its reality? Was I on Mini-Thins back then, too? Was I? Did that stuff scramble my brain even back then, before this happened? We may just be in for some unbearably harsh terrain here I'm afraid, under thunderstorming skies.

Everything in my field of vision is hazy, in soft focus, grainy grey. Strange medical-looking machines with blinking lights are scattered around this place, occasionally making eerie beeping noises. The windows seem covered in cellophane or acid rain-streaks.

Cuba? Why Cuba?

My body looks down. Tan T-shirt and dog tags. Good. Okay. A slight stench of body odor covered with the faint smell of camouflage-painted skin, bloody gauze, white medical tape, plastic tubes, and Lysol. Okay. My mind feels like someone is suffocating it somehow, suppressing the free flow of thought. It doesn't exactly ache, it just feels strangled, like everything is an effort—thinking, breathing, everything. I feel exhausted, used up, worn out. My legs and ass and back all feel achy and painful. My left arm pulsates in a way that makes it seem like something is being piped into my body. I also have this vague, nagging sense that I have to pee. It isn't overwhelming to the point of discomfort, but it's just kind of there, like the way a slight over-pull on a riser can completely ruin your landing. It's manageable, but still. I peek my eyes around and can't easily tell where the latrine door is.

My mind conjures a thought about why in the world I'd agreed to be Airborne. Some stupid recruiting trick? Promises of glory? Of seventy-two virgins? My mind can't remember exactly, beyond Horndecker and Neebs urging me to join with them, beyond the promised glory of joining the ranks of the warrior-writers. My brain just doesn't seem to have ready access to that information. Something about more monthly money, and something about jump boots. Why do I care about wearing jump boots? Jump boots?

Jump boots or jungle boots? Cuba?

My mind can't seem to perceive time correctly. Everything is out of focus, tilted, changed, different, *off*. My body feels a bone-chilling fear, even though it seems to be relatively safe. My body feels, oddly, insecure, like everything previously reliable was now open to curious investigation.

The fatigue itself is proving to be a formidable opponent. My mind seems to insist on trying to determine how my body got here, *here*, to this bed, with these threadbare sheets and decades-old, scratchy, olive-drab blankets. Trying to remember feels like slogging through a 20-mile ruck march in a pouring, piercing North Carolina hail of pin-pricks.

My mind remembers my body being wheeled in—parked, on a...stretcher?—in a hallway with its ankle pulsing in radiating pain. My mind thought, too, that they left me there for a long time, waiting and scared and anxious. My body had never broken a bone before, and this felt like a kind of serious neither my mind nor my body had any familiarity with. The drugs weren't helping. The Mini-Thins, that is. My mind almost always chose that brand of ephedrine, Mini-Thins, when I needed to be an "Army of One." The combination of whatever painkillers the medic shot me up with on the drop zone and the Minis must have worn off amid the extreme fatigue and the adrenaline drop in the ambulance, making recollections that much harder.

At some point—my mind is sure I'm mixing things up here, but at some point—my body drifted back into sleep, then half-awoke and saw what looked like a familiar ghost. It looked like my father, with his full brown, bristly beard, and his middle-aged ring of hair around his otherwise bald head. He was wearing his square-lensed reading glasses. He looked like he was reading something and my mind assumed it was the Bible, because that would be the most likely book for him to be reading. He liked the contradictions in it, "puzzles" he called them, to work out in his mind. If this was the word of God, he said, then clearly any seeming contradictions were the result of poor human interpretation of the words, rather than with the words themselves. As far as my mind knew, he hadn't solved any of these puzzles yet. My mind thought he probably enjoyed working on them more than any joy he'd get from solving them.

He flashed—flickered—in and out of my vision, like an old rabbit-eared television struggling to get reception. My body couldn't help but feel some of the feelings it *always* felt when it saw my father: a deep-set anxiety at the core of its solar plexus, accompanied by pangs of guilt, shame, and regret. It was painful, and so much of a burden that mind would *try* to avoid feeling these things by wandering off onto some weird tangent. It didn't work, usually, but my mind sure tried like hell.

"Where do these feelings come from?" my mind thought. "How do they get here if I don't think them into existence? Must be some kind of instinctual mechanism, beyond my ability for understanding." How odd, for this to be triggered by the sight of one's own father. How disadvantageous. How crippling.

My body blinks my eyes and my father disappears. My body blinks again, and a blurry image starts to appear, but my mind can't quite tell what it is. My body laid my head back on the pillow, closed my eyes, and the hospital room disappears, replaced by an open, grassy field. "Don't you quit on me, Kronos!" a high-pitched, male voice screams, from nowhere. "Don't you quit on me!"

I kept trying to get my brain to render the truth but it just kept sputtering and spitting out silly madness. What diabolical tricks had afflicted it? Where did they emanate from? One can hardly understand these things in the cold light of reason, in the cold eyes of objective assessment. A break seems natural. There are only *some* pieces of the puzzle that are even visible, let alone *knowable*. Somehow I knew, or thought, Neebs and Horndecker were gone, but I didn't even know how I thought I knew that.

What the hell *happened?* My mind remembered the C-130, the loud rumbling, pounding, overbearing of the cabin interior. My mind remembered being packed in on the bench-seat next to Neebs on my right, and Horndecker on my left. Despite the Minis in my system, my body insisted on trying to get some sleep between wheels-up and stand-up. My mind dreamed of

Jenny, about watching a movie on her tan couch with her black miniature schnauzer, Benny. Jenny and Benny. I thought about Benny hopping out of an airplane with a little red parachute on his back, his snout-beard flittering in the wind like a jellyfish through sea-water. He'd be fine, my mind thought in its sleepy sleeplessness. Of course. Instincts would take over. Animal survival skills. No problem. High speed, low drag, hoo-ah.

My mind sometimes did that. Played tricks. It tried to cope, I guess, with how exactly it got deceived into believing that jumping from airplanes was a good way to spend the best parts of your mid-20's. It seemed impossible, yet *was*, and so silly fictions needed to be conjured. A schnauzer with a tiny Kevlar helmet and a parachute rippling above him as he floated down toward the drop zone. Somehow, this seemed to be the right image for my mind to conjure in the moments before the action started. Nothing but delusions on top of delusions on top of delusions.

My mind wants to go back, to research the reasons, to figure out *why*. Why was my body in this hospital? Because my body got injured on a jump. Why did my body get injured on a jump? Because my body landed wrong. Why did my body land wrong? Because my brain misjudged the distance to the ground and my body misadjusted my stance. And why did that happen? Because the Mini-Thins were affecting my judgment. And why did my body take Mini-Thins...

My father's face flickered into view again, followed by Drill Sergeant Duza's in his ridiculous drill sergeant hat, his clean-shaven face red from spending twelve Basic Training hours a day in the Oklahoma sun.

My brain flashed back again to my childhood room. My father was reading to me from Thomas Aquinas, from *Summa Theologica*. "I answer that, It was necessary for man's salvation that there should be a knowledge revealed by God besides philosophical science built up by human reason. Firstly, indeed, because man is directed to God, as to an end that surpasses the grasp of his reason..." That kind of stuff. "The God Bullshit," as they said in *Network*. Where is the clarity that my mind needed? These books, these movies, they've failed me, it seems.

My father, he read these books. During our reading time at night, he was still in his resplendent white collar, wearing his scholarly spectacles, and always presented an earnest look on his face. He read with a deep, resonant voice full of certitude and emotion, such that the words, and the very act of reading itself, became ingrained in my faulty mind as sacred.

My body blinks again.

Now my body was in Drill Sergeant Duza's office. He said, "That's ridiculous, Specialist Kronos."

"Drill Sergeant, I just don't have the temperament for this, Drill Sergeant," my voice said.

"No," he said. "You're not quitting, that's the end of it."

"Drill Sergeant, I'll go smoke a joint in front of the first sergeant. This just isn't my thing, Drill Sergeant."

He rushed from behind his desk and got in my face. "Kronos, you *will* not quit on me! I'll be on your ass every damned day, and that's that! I will not let you quit! I will fix these dog-gone temperament issues of yours, Specialist. I'll swear on a stack of Bibles on that, son."

My mind fades out the memory, or delusion, or scene from an off-Broadway play, or whatever it was.

My body blinks and my mind nods off into the blankness of sleep again.

11.

Writing from the Ruins:

An Unreliable History of Postmodern Literary Fiction

1. Introduction

Postmodern literature defies a simple, coherent definition. The beginning, middle, and end of the movement—just as the stories which it contains—cannot easily be marked. Rather than clearly designated points on a timeline, postmodern literature exists as a sort of blur somewhere between the modernist movement and contemporary literature. Regardless, there are some tentative markers used for the sake of discussion and there is a definite historical context in which we can trace the emergence of this defiant literary movement. What is, perhaps, more useful to understand, however, are the literary features which characterize postmodern literature as well as the landmark authors and works which exemplify such features. For a full understanding of the movement, then, we must understand the historical context in which it is embedded; the style and literary techniques which distinguish it from others; and the key types of works which can be found within it.

2. The Historical Context

One simply cannot discuss the history of postmodern literature without first understanding that the genre is, as Umberto Eco famously said, a "transhistorical" phenomenon. That is, it cannot easily be confined to a specific historical period and, furthermore, it is not best understood in such temporal terms. Postmodernism is, above all else, a literary style, not a period of time.

However, with that said, for the purposes of discussing the movement, 1941 is frequently used as a rough marker for the beginnings of postmodernism as this is the year in which both James Joyce and Virginia Woolf—both key figures of modernism—died. Others, however, site the first publication of *The Cannibal* by John Hawkes in 1949 as the beginning since this is considered by many to be the first published novel in the style of postmodern literature. Thus, postmodernism emerges in the wake of the traumatic second world war; including the holocaust, the Japanese American internment camps; the atomic bombing of both Hiroshima and Nagasaki; and all the other horrendous human rights violations perpetrated during these years. Such events linger in our collective consciousness to this day. After the war ended, the world was launched into the tense, anxiety-riddled cold war in which the threat of global nuclear devastation loomed over everyone. At the same time—and rightly so—tradition was being challenged by the multiple civil rights movements which popped up mid-Century.

In their own troubled way, postmodern literary techniques can be seen as attempting through art to process or respond to the world in which it now finds itself. Throughout its unstable and fragmented narratives, readers often find strong political messages or critiques of the socioeconomic environment in which the authors lived. While modernist literature also challenged the conventions of its day and, in many ways, exhibits a strong sense of alienation from the mainstream public sphere, postmodernism is "founded...in the ruins of the public sphere" (Clark, 148). That is, the literature does not attempt to exist on the margins of its historical context but rather, deeply embedded in the chaos and fragmentation which it saw in its historical context.

3. The Postmodern Narrative and its Key Figures and Works

It is worth bearing in mind, however, that not all literature produced after the second world war can be accurately categorized as postmodern fiction. There were and are other literary movements which occurred parallel to the postmodern movement. This is one of the reasons why strictly defining the literature by a historical period as we tend to do with other movements is so particularly problematic here. Postmodern literature, more than others, relies on style and literary techniques to convey its narrative as much or more than it relies on any actual plot or story. Thus, readers will often find more meaning in *how* a postmodern narrative is written than *what* it is actually about. For this reason then, it is, perhaps, better understood by its unique stylistic qualities and literary techniques. One might be tempted to say "form" but, as will soon become apparent, such a term is too rigid a category for the postmodern narrative.

To generalize broadly about the style of the postmodern narrative, one could say that it can be characterized by irony or playfulness, pastiche or intertextuality, fragmentation, chaos, metafiction, temporal distortion, hyper-reality, magic realism, paranoia, maximalism, minimalism, and/or the problematic of representation. Even with this list of techniques and characteristics, it is not quite clear exactly what a postmodern narrative looks like. For that, it is necessary to achieve a more comprehensive understanding of each term—many of which were coined retrospectively while attempting to nail down just what makes a narrative postmodern.

3.1 Irony or Playfulness

The playfulness of both the language and structure of postmodernist fiction is often cited as its most characteristic feature. While one can, of course, find humor and irony in other works, it is a near ubiquitous feature of postmodernism. Postmodern authors like Joseph Heller and Kurt Vonnegut are famous for the playful ways in which they deal with serious subjects like war and other atrocities. Such playfulness emerges in the form of wordplay, ironic narratives or ironic structure, and a generally light or humorous tone when discussing the serious topics which pervaded postwar society.

3.2 Pastiche or "Intertextuality"

As with playfulness, pastiche also characterizes almost every narrative which falls under the category of postmodern. The term implies a "pasting together" of multiple elements. In literary theory, it is often also referred to as a bricolage—a term originally applied to the visual arts and referring to the construction of a work from an eclectic range of resources. In literature, then, this most often takes the form of references to other texts or other media often in homage or as a parody of the referenced text. (While many authors who cannot be considered postmodern are inspired by or borrow elements from other authors and other works, it is done more bluntly in postmodern literature.) That is, the different pieces, when "pasted" together, do not necessarily form a cohesive whole. The reader is usually made very aware that other texts or media are being referenced. Because the pieces do not quite fit, the reader is left with an unresolved sense of the plurality and chaos which characterize contemporary society. One landmark work which exemplifies this is *Naked Lunch* by William S Burroughs. This is a fractured narrative which combines elements of detective fiction, science fiction, and westerns to tell the paranoid and hallucinatory tale of a drug addict (a topic not typical to any of the three genres mentioned.)

Whereas pastiche refers more to borrowing various elements and pasting them together, intertextuality is used to discuss the relationships between texts and the ways in which they reference each other. While the modernist narrative can often be read as isolated—alienated, even—from the rest of the world in which it was created, postmodernist literature is acutely aware of how embedded it is in its sociopolitical and historical context. Authors will make direct references or very clear allusions to other works, including previous or future works by that very same author (self-referentialism.) In this way, postmodern literature is intertextual and it becomes increasingly important for the reader to be familiar with all the works referenced in order to arrive at more fully developed interpretations.

3.3 Fragmentation

Fragmentation can occur along many lines in postmodern literature. The plot, characters, narration, imagery, themes, and all other elements of the story can be fragmented. It can even occur in the language, grammar, or structure of the text. A sequence of events might be interrupted; the timeline might be nonlinear or cut up and rearranged; words might be missing; or whole pages might be blank. *Giovanni's Room* by James Baldwin offers an excellent example of a fragmented plotline. The story of a man attempting to reconcile his past and his true desires is told in a broken narrative about his struggle to choose between two lovers (a man whom he truly loves and a woman who could offer him the conventional "happy" lifestyle). The plot—which is already nonlinear—is broken apart and spliced with pieces of the past.

3.4 Chaos

Weighty tomes and dissertations have been written on the ways in which postmodernism embraces chaos. Joseph Conte even goes so far as to argue that the genre can be compared with chaos theory in the sense that it "dispenses with modernism's binary distinction and hierarchy of order/disorder, replacing it with an attitude resembling the two primary branches of chaos theory, which investigate 'order as the possible emanation of disorder, and chaos as one possible result of an overly stringent order—the process by which one becomes the other" (Conte in Ebbesen, 192). In simpler terms, postmodernism blurs the boundary between order and disorder by conflating them both as processes of chaos. Unlike the modernist, the postmodernist embraces this chaos. Hence, postmodern authors are regarded as writing "in the ruins" as Clark mentioned earlier. Chaotic narratives lack any decipherable timeline or cohesive plotline. The legendary poem, *Howl*, by Allen Ginsberg is the perfect example of chaos in postmodernism. The language of the poem has a certain spontaneity which is sometimes academic, sometimes colloquial, sometimes another tone altogether. The point of view shifts along with the identity of the narrator. The very structure of the poem alters throughout so that it becomes an incongruous pastiche of poetic form. (Another example of this kind of poem—even though it was written in the modernist "era"—*The Waste Land* by T.S. Eliot.) Out of this disorder emerges a beautiful (if not quite ordered) poem that has become one of the prime examples of postmodern style.

3.5 Metafiction

The prefix "meta" refers to the self-conscious way in which a work draws attention to itself. Metafiction, then, is a literary device which directly points out the fictional nature of fiction. This device turns the entire concept of "suspension of disbelief" on its head and undermines the authority of narrative conventions. Metafiction is used for a variety of reasons. An author might want to parody the form; identify the limitations of representation in literature; or simply reflect on various aspects of fiction. The technique can be found in many postmodern novels but it is, perhaps, most interesting in *Slaughterhouse Five* by Kurt Vonnegut. The novel begins with the author describing the process of writing the novel and continues to refer to himself throughout. Although the story is about a real event which the author personally experienced himself—the completely unnecessary fire-bombing of Dresden, Germany—it features many clearly fictional elements like extraterrestrials and time travel. In this way, Vonnegut is calling attention to the inability to adequately represent lived experience in fiction (a concept which will be discussed in further detail below).

3.6 Temporal Distortion

Temporal distortion refers to more than just the fragmentation of timelines and nonlinear storytelling. It also refers to the common usage of anachronisms in postmodern fiction. Historical elements might blend with fictional elements or historical events or figures which occurred far apart from each other might be conflated. Time in the postmodern narrative overlaps, repeats itself, or split suddenly into multiple directions. This opens up the narrative to many possibilities and allows meaning to be conveyed beyond the conventional, linear timeline of cause followed by effect.

3.7 Hyperreality

Hyperreality is a term which refers to the inability to distinguish actual reality from a simulated or artificial reality. Rather than an individual deficiency, this is treated by postmodernism as the general condition of humanity in our increasingly mediated, or media-saturated lives. Rather than attempting to discover or represent any true reality, then, postmodern literature reflects this condition of hyperreality through narratives which blur the boundaries between illusion and real experience. Don DeLillo's *White Noise* deals extensively with hyperreality as it explores the media saturation of modern life along with many other themes in a characteristically postmodern style. The movie *The Matrix* also deals with this theme successfully.

3.8 Magic Realism

The term "magic realism" may appear oxymoronic at first glance. However, it refers to the more surrealist elements of postmodern fiction. The technique was originally developed in Latin America and was made famous by Jorge Luis Borges and his famous work *Historia Universal de la Infamia* (*A Universal History of Infamy*.) In this seminal work, Borges tells fictional narratives about real criminals. In these narratives, readers gain a sense of the dream-like, surreal nature of magic realism which juxtaposes or wholly conflates realistic and fantastic elements. Gabriel Garcia Marquez is another acclaimed author in this area.

3.9 Paranoia

Paranoia in postmodern literature is closely associated with conceptions of order. That is, where paranoia is present, it is due to the underlying belief that some sinister order is at the bottom of the chaos which is found in the world. Because postmodernism already deals so heavily with chaos and the problematic binary of order/disorder, paranoia as a literary device was a natural development. It permeates the works of William S. Burroughs whose novels reflect the convoluted, distorted, and paranoid perspective of drug addicts and other subjugated members of society.

3.10 Maximalism

Maximalism is, perhaps, best understood as a reaction against minimalism. However, both techniques can be found in postmodernism so it is inaccurate to say that the one excludes the other. It calls into question the role of the narrative in literature and, as with many postmodern literary devices, brings style to the forefront. Evidence of this device can be found in famous works such as *On the Road* by Jack Kerouac in which the narrative contains elaborate detail along with frequent digressions and reference. The goal with maximalism is to build a literary style which reflects the narrative in a way that conventional literary devices cannot accomplish. See also: *Infinite Jest* by David Foster Wallace.

3.11 Minimalism

The other side of that coin, then, is minimalism which is characterized by sparse description, leaving the reader to fill in the rest of the details. Rather than thoroughly describing the scene, the reader is given vague suggestions or innuendos which must be interpreted. Through this technique, the possibilities for interpretation become multiplied. Like maximalism, it can be used to more accurately reflect the narrative. Great examples of minimalism can be found in the many works of Charles Bukowski. *Cause and Effect,* for example, is a poem told in nine short lines with few adjectives or adverbs. Through this minimalist style, Bukowski builds an image of suicide from both the perspective of those who commit suicide and those whom they leave behind.

3.12 The Problematic of Representation

In addition to such literary techniques and stylistic tendencies as have been described up until this point, there is also in every postmodern work an overarching sense that experience cannot be adequately represented. Rather, it can only be referenced, alluded to, or suggested. As part of our everyday lives in modern society, "representations such as film, television, and the internet, in many cases, constitute primary life experiences. Thus, experiences through media become more real than the experiences encountered in day-to-day life" (Meacham & Buendia, 512). As a consequence, authors and literary critics alike began to experience "crises of representation" and attempted to draw attention to them without necessarily resolving them (Clark, 149). This is accomplished both by these characteristically postmodern techniques (particularly, fragmentation, temporal distortion, hyperreality and metafiction) as well as the very apparent lack of a conventional plot line or resolution. Language (the mode of representation in literature) has a tendency to break down in the postmodern narrative. Words are detached from their meanings or remade and given new meanings or associations. As Jameson argues in Clark, there is "a linguistic malfunction, a detachment of signifier from signified, a disruption of personal identity as it is constituted in a temporal unification of past, present, and future. The 'active temporal unification' at stake...'is itself a function of language'; it is what enables both selfhood as we know it and storytelling" (Clark, 149). In this way, the reader is made aware of the irreconcilable distance between the signifier and the signified as well as the inability of language to perfectly capture and unify the temporality (the past, present, and future) of an experience. Rather than acting as a representation of experience, then, the postmodern narrative is more accurately understood as a *reflection* of experience. That is, an imperfect, distorted, and subjective account—a sort of anti-narrative—of real, lived experiences.

4. Conclusion

As the stylistic elements and literary devices changed or were deployed in new ways over time, a concurrent shift in the way in which readers approached these narratives also occurred. The reader of postmodern fiction cannot passively absorb the narrative. Instead, the narrative demands—through the use of these various unique literary devices—that it be actively engaged and interpreted. The existence of multiple possible interpretations require the reader to deconstruct and take apart the narrative in order to arrive at these interpretations. Furthermore, the intertextuality of postmodern fiction means the reader must be aware of other texts which are being referenced.

Such a complex and multifaceted genre as postmodernism, of course, came with its critics who often argued that the narratives were too intricate and confusing. Despite criticism, however, the movement persisted. Postmodernism experienced a peak or "golden age" around the middle of the 20th century but it did not end there. There are many contemporary authors such as David Foster Wallace, Jennifer Egan, Chuck Palahniuk, Zadi Smith, Neil Gaiman, and Giannina Braschi who are widely regarded as being representative of a continued postmodern literary movement. With its characteristically experimental and defiant style keeping it ever fresh and new, it is no surprise that postmodernism has endured as an important and powerful artistic movement.

Works Cited

Clark, Miriam. "Contemporary Short Fiction and the Postmodern Condition." *Studies in Short Fiction* 32.2 (1995): 147-154. Print.

Ebbesen, Jeffrey. "Design and Debris: A Chaotics of Postmodern American Fiction (review)." *College Literature* 32.2 (2005): 192-194. Print.

Meacham, Shuaib J, and Edward Buendia. "Modernism, Postmodernism, and Post-Structuralism and Their Impact on Literacy." *Language Arts* 76.6 (1999): 510-516. Print.

Sinha, Adya. "Fragmentation and Postmodernism I." *Examiner.com*. N.p., 20 Sept. 2011. Web. 2 July 2014. www.examiner.com/article/fragmentation-and-postmodernism-i.

12.

Moving Beyond Ayn Rand:

Why Postmodernism is the Most Effective Literary Genre for Advancing Libertarian Ideas

I. Introduction

Within the vast expanse of literature that has been produced over the past few decades and which can be characterized as postmodern, readers find a wide range of ideas that can come into conflict with each other and themselves. Citizens of these modern times are faced with a fragmented and sometimes polarized environment in which it can be difficult to find one's bearings and make sense of those many conflicting ideas. However, by immersing oneself in literature of the postmodern genre, the reader can begin to gain a foothold. This genre of literature lends itself particularly well to the expression of political ideas and especially those newer and more nuanced political ideas such as libertarianism.

Authors of postmodern literature have a wide range of literary tools at their disposal in order to advance convincing and influential political arguments. Before taking a closer look at how postmodern fiction can be effectively deployed in order to create a more libertarian society, one must first have a better understanding of postmodernism, libertarianism, and how beliefs—especially political beliefs—are influenced by fiction.

II. A Brief Analysis of Postmodern Literature

Postmodernism emerged amid the backdrop of the second world war and the emergence of an anxiety-ridden Cold War landscape. However, postmodernism defies a clear historical placement. It is a literary movement unrestricted by any specific time period (nor, in fact, the concept of time itself.) This is evidenced by the fact that it continues today, evolving and adapting to the sociocultural climate in which it finds itself.

Even though it does not belong to a specific time period, we can see clear influences from important historical events such as World War II—including its traumatic events such as Japanese-American internment, atomic bombings, the holocaust, and other comparably horrific human rights violations. Postmodern literature deals with these traumatic past events in the context of society's present collective anxieties and fears. Individual crises of identity mingle with global politics and radical ideas and demands for civil rights, creating a complex and sometimes fragmented work of literature like Allen Ginsberg's *Howl* or William S. Burroughs's *Naked Lunch*.

In this way, we can understand postmodernism's reliance on techniques such as playfulness, pastiche, magic realism, paranoia, metafiction, temporal distortion, and others as attempts to process or, at the very least, better express the modern human experience. Where the traditional methods of narration failed to adequately capture the reality in which postmodern authors now found themselves, these new techniques became indispensable tools for building a new narrative which better captured the essence of modernity.

Readers of postmodern literature are exposed to both new challenges and new avenues for interpretation, allowing for the spread of ideas with greater complexity as well as the inclusion of more subtle—and often overlooked—nuances contained within those ideas. The style endures not only because its many different techniques allow for a near endless amount of new and unique works but also because it allows for the story to capture that experience of reality beyond clear-cut, black and white terms. The time in which we find ourselves does not lend itself easily to clearly defined boundaries of right and wrong. Perhaps, no time period ever really did. But, with the advent of postmodernism, the complexity of life—and, particularly, the complexity of human experience—can now be better captured by the written word.

This opens up (blows open?) the door for a wide range of possibilities. The literary techniques developed by postmodernism can be deployed in a number of interesting and powerful ways in order to convey social, cultural, or political ideals.

III. A Brief Analysis of Libertarianism

While the modern form of libertarianism (in the shape of the Libertarian Party of the United States of America, sometimes called "Big L Libertarianism") only goes back to 1971 when it was founded by a small group of individuals including David Nolan, its roots go back as far as the Enlightenment of the 17th Century. Writers like John Locke and Thomas Paine of this era became a strong influence on the modern social, political, and economic ideals of libertarianism. The ideas of these early proto-libertarian authors were so influential, in fact, that they helped form some of the most basic principles upon which the United States Constitution is founded. Locke's individualistic ideals, for example, can be found in the historical Declaration of Independence which asserted the right of the people to change or abolish a government which no longer protected their rights or freedoms.

Although we can find many strong libertarian threads in these important documents, it is not entirely accurate to call the founding fathers or the United States government necessarily purely libertarian. The encyclopedia defines libertarianism as a political philosophy which:

> "takes individual liberty to be the primary political value....Liberalism seeks to define and justify the legitimate powers of government in terms of certain natural or God-given individual rights. These rights include the rights to life, liberty, private property,

> freedom of speech and association, freedom of worship, government by consent, equality under the law, and moral autonomy (the pursuit of one's own conception of happiness, or the "good life.") The purpose of government, according to liberals, is to protect these and other individual rights...They contend that the scope and powers of government should be constrained so as to allow each individual as much freedom of action as is consistent with a like freedom for everyone else. Thus, they believe that individuals should be free to behave and to dispose of their property as they see fit, provided that their actions do not infringe on the equal freedom of others." (*Encyclopedia Britannica*)
>
> *NOTE: The above definition is often referred to today as "classical liberalism," as opposed to the kind of liberalism practiced by the Democrat Party in the modern-day United States.*

In sum, libertarianism advocates a limited government whose sole purpose is to ensure the freedoms of its individual citizens. In order to do so, the government should not interfere in the lives of citizens beyond what is necessary to make sure that no one citizen is infringing on the freedoms or rights of other citizens. In addition, different strands of libertarianism exist regarding exactly what role the government should play within a society. Some argue more from the economic position of low to no taxes and a laissez-faire economy while others argue from a more social perspective of personal autonomy and freedom of choice (limiting the scope of the law only to those crimes which cause demonstrable harm to others.) Still others argue for a more socialistic state which protects its citizens from exploitation while still allowing them individual freedoms. No matter which strand of libertarian philosophy one belongs to, however, the basic ideals of personal autonomy, civil liberties, and limited functions of the government are consistent throughout.

IV. Postmodernism as a Tool of Libertarian Ideas

With these basic understandings of postmodern fiction and libertarian ideals in place, the intersection and relationships between the two can start to become clearer. Many of the principles of libertarianism can be seen embedded in the very form that postmodernist fiction takes. However, in order to better understand what advantage this provides to libertarian authors, we must first understand how fiction influences its readers more broadly.

1. The Influence of Fiction on Beliefs and Human Behavior

In recent years, more and more attention has been paid to the effect fiction has on how we form our beliefs and ideas about the world around us. An astonishing amount of research has show that we do, in many surprising ways, incorporate fictional narratives and fictional events into our understandings of the real world around us. In fact, "a series of laboratory experiments have shown that viewers, after they were exposed to fictional narratives, confused fact with fiction and drew from fictional information when answering knowledge questions about the actual world." (Mulligan & Habel, 2-3.)

While this can, in some cases, have negative consequences, for the most part this is a positive finding. It shows that humans have the unique ability to incorporate experiences they have not personally had into informed opinions. While it is important to separate fact from fiction in general, this is a great evolutionary advantage for humanity. One does not have to personally experience global nuclear war, for example, to make the informed decision that it should be avoided at all costs. In the case of politics, one can learn from fictional accounts what the potential negative effects of, say, a loss of basic freedoms might be without needing to experience those negative effects personally.

Thus, fiction provides a powerful medium that, when used in the right way, can promote understanding and empathy within and across societies so that individuals can make informed decisions to move toward a better ideal of government, or social order in a broader sense. As Mulligan and Habel argue,

"Entertainment media can expand our horizons and introduce us vicariously to new feelings and experiences—all without leaving our homes. While viewers likely approach fiction mindful of its shortcomings, they also know it can provide lessons for real life." (Mulligan & Habel, 2.) A well-written narrative can effectively instill a certain set of morals and political ideas in the reader's mind. In some cases, fiction can be even more effective than real life as readers are less skeptical or reluctant to accept fictional narratives than, say, outright political arguments or opinions.

2. The Case of Postmodernist Fiction and Libertarianism

To understand this specifically in the context of libertarian ideals, then, one can begin to see how postmodern techniques and literary styles lend themselves particularly well to the formation of convincing fictional narratives which promote libertarian political concepts. Through the use of techniques such as irony, magic realism, pastiche, metafiction, temporal distortion, and others a libertarian author can create a uniquely libertarian tone.

For example, with irony, the author can poke fun of or call attention to the downfalls of real-world governments or societies. With temporal distortion, the author can play with historical timelines by describing alternate outcomes of major historical events or placing important historical figures in different time periods. Through the use of pastiche, an author can create a mosaic fictional society pulling from elements of real societies all around the world or across all of "time." With metafiction, the author is opened up to a variety of possibilities. For example, she could frame an expressly fictional narration within a real one or vice versa. Unlike magic realism, the author can create an ideal utopia or a daunting dystopia (or a combination of both) which can provide an allegory for contemporary society or a clear vision of what the libertarian ideal would look like.

Perhaps more than any other genre, then, postmodern fiction is uniquely suited to the task of expressing libertarian ideas in a way that helps maintain the many nuances and complexities of those ideas. Furthermore, it provides a medium of expression for these ideas that is, in many cases, more influential than traditional forms of political expression such as debates, arguments, or stating public opinion polls as the audience of fiction is less resistant to the thoughts and ideas embedded in the postmodern fictional work.

V. Conclusion

Fiction has long been a powerful medium for both expressing and spreading beliefs and ideas. This is one of the reasons we can find so many incidents throughout history of book burning, censorship, and the outright banning of certain "dangerous" books. If the written word were not as influential as it is, and therefore as big a threat to the powers that be as it is, none of these things would ever occur.

As with any stylistic movement, certain political, cultural, or social ideals become inextricably linked with the various stylistic tendencies and forms in the literature of the day. Those found in postmodernism are uniquely positioned to express libertarian ideals better than any other literary movement in history. This is because influence begins first with a widening of the mind horizon of the target of influence. Postmodernism is well-positioned to be able to do just that in a subtle manner, such that the principles of libertarianism can then be considered without the defenses of mainstream social conditioning being triggered.

Works Cited

Clark, Miriam. "Contemporary Short Fiction and the Postmodern Condition." *Studies in Short Fiction* 32.2 (1995): 146-154. Print.

Ebbesen, Jeffrey. "Design and Debris: A Chaotics of Postmodern American Fiction (review)." *College Literature* 32.2 (2005): 192-194. Print.

"libertarianism." *Encyclopaedia Britannica. Encyclopaedia Britannica Online Academic Edition*. Encyclopaedia Britannica, Inc., 2014. Web. 15 July 2014. <http://www.britannica.com/EB-

checked/topic/339321/libertarianism>.

Meacham, Shuaib J., and Buendia, Edward. "Modernism, Postmodernism, and Post-Structuralism and Their Impact on Literacy." *Language Arts* 76.6 (1999): 510-516. Print.

Mulligan, K., and Habel, P. "The Implications of Fictional Media for Political Beliefs." *American Politics Research* 41.1 (2012): 122-46. Web.

About the Author

Frank Marcopolos once ate a hot sauce so hot the restaurant made him sign a waiver before they would serve it to him. No kidding. He has a witness.

His other published works include:

Almost Home
A Car Crash of Sorts
The Whirligig: Issues 3 – 9

He also hosts a literary-themed podcast, "Saturday Show," which can be found at his personal website, FrankMarcopolos.com, as well as on iTunes and Stitcher.

Frank lives in Austin, Texas with his pet tetra, Fredward. He is on Twitter and Facebook.

Critical acclaim for his work includes the following:

"I read "Almost Home" in one sitting. (All right, I ate breakfast, lunch, and dinner but after fixing them, I read while I ate. Usually I resist this temptation if the book's on my Kindle.) But "Almost Home" keeps you in its thrall. The language rings true—and reads seamlessly within each character's alternating chapters. The vivid atmosphere settled me in a sleepy burg where the cultural and social center was the college. The powerful and vivid atmosphere, much the same as when I was in college, although much more hypnotic and alluring, goes further. It seduces one to remain on the cusp of adulthood forever. In "Almost Home" that powerful temptation seems possible—at the price of selling one's soul."

– Kathleen Maher, review on Amazon.com

"Marcopolos takes us from the barracks to the couch of a Delta Force captain—not at home—whose wife Dante met "through the plausible guise of Amway." There's Dante's attempt to connect with another soldier jumping from a C-130. Also a drunken drive down the North Carolina backroads. Through it all, Dante struggles against the feeling that he is under bombardment and it's "only a matter of time before they [get] the coordinates right and [nail him] with a direct hit." He needs to move. He craves action, but he's leery when it comes. Marcopolos riffs on the rhythms of real-guy speech. He punctuates his straight-up style with the occasional over-the-top phrase or reference. His soldiers' voices are right on. He shows us military life as only an insider can. And he makes us feel for this soldier who struggles to leave his demons and his isolation behind."

– Barr Bielinski, review on Amazon.com

CPSIA information can be obtained at www.ICGtesting.com
Printed in the USA
LVOW12s2324161214

419056LV00002B/2/P

9 780983 459996